The House on the Cliff

BY THE SAME AUTHOR

The Scapegoat: A Life of Moses (novel)

JOAN LAWRENCE

The House on the Cliff

PETER OWEN · LONDON

ISBN 0 7206 0763 9

Illustrations by Louis Mackay

PETER OWEN PUBLISHERS
73 Kenway Road London SW5 0RE

First published in Great Britain 1989
© Joan Lawrence 1989

Printed in Great Britain by WBC Bristol and Maesteg

For
Cecil and Pat Bourne

What is this life if, full of care,
We have no time to stand and stare.

W.H. Davies

We are the Pilgrims, we shall go
  Always a little further: it may be
Beyond that last blue mountain barred with snow,
  Across that angry or that glimmering sea . . .

James Elroy Flecker

Contents

— 1 —

Incomer or White Settler?

The house was a ruin. No question. I peered into it doubtfully, yet with the same enthusiasm I had felt on so many similar occasions, my head and my heart ever in violent competition, each trying to govern the other. How well I knew from previous, and not always satisfactory, experience, which would win! So I took myself in hand, quelling that spurt of exhilaration, determined to give proper weight to all the disadvantages.

Disadvantages? Well yes, they were all too obvious. Battered ridges of rusty corrugated iron constituted a dubious roof; black holes gaped where windows once had shone. Inside, a door or two hung disconsolately from broken hinges, while innocent-looking floor-boards offered sudden gaps within which to trap the unwary. Apart from an old bedstead and a few mysterious and apparently immovable objects, there was evidence of smaller residents, both feathered and furred, having rather more immediacy than the lingering traces of long-departed humans. Pigeons' droppings dripped over convenient shelving which might have been expressly designed for their comfort. Mouse dirt abounded. There was a smell of cosy nests. Other, more subtle emanations, which might have warned of both stoats and weasels, could, however, have been detected only if the smeller had been more experienced in such matters.

The fireplace in this long-abandoned coastguard house was a battered iron range, and no encouragement was to be

9

had from noting that twin streams of water, seeping in from a now non-existent chimney, had stained the surrounding walls – rather like a faded medieval fresco – into distinct images of white-robed angels. But perhaps my heart did leap just a little, since I am partial to angels. They were indeed tall and majestic, flanking the rusted grate with sudden promise, arms beckoning and wings spread wide across the dirt-distempered walls. Was this then an invitation? Could I rely on it? But also, and perhaps rather more to the point, those walls were certainly massive: great blocks of dressed grey stone, two feet thick and built to last under a government which, back in 1906, had known just how such work should be done.

Around this derelict house, a garden, equally derelict, ran between the end of farmland and the edge of a wild northern cliff. Or at least, if not actually what could be called a garden, then a piece of rough cliff-top which gave some hope of becoming one. There was even a wood, a stand of *Pinus contorta*, offering sanctuary to a mixed and not altogether harmonious crowd of small birds. Presumably it had been planted – though without effect, as I was to discover – as protection against the savage storm-force easterlies of winter. Well, yes. On that soft spring evening of 1976 I could not possibly have imagined the violence, if not from the east then from the roaring west, which would at times pick me up and roll me down the slope.

I made my way through the tangled grass, stepping carefully around lumps of iron whose purposes had long since been forgotten, and avoiding so far as possible the ancient cans and bottles which lay (as I discovered when digging them up) in a neat semicircle near the back door, indicating the extent of the thrower's 'fetch'. The cliff, I discovered with relief, fell away gently; no plunging rock-face to frighten me off for ever. It was grassed and whin-clad, crossed at different levels by narrow sheep-trods and with wider tracks dropping to the water. Below, spreading between the cliff's out-thrusting buttresses and the sea itself, lay a wide, sheep-bitten, herb-starred, grassy shore, ending in a barrier of rocks. This, though I did not then know it, was an early raised beach, released about ten thousand years ago from the incredible pressure of retreating glaciers. Scotland, with gaps between the Ice Ages, had lain centuries' long beneath the vast ice-sheets that crept implacably from the western mountains and across the flatter areas of Easter Ross, challenging at last the other glaciers from Norway in the shallow plain which is now the North Sea. The battle that ensued must have been tremendous, as huge armies of slow-moving ice met each other head on: apparently a clear case of an irresistible force meeting an immovable object. But in the end a truce was called, and 'our' glacier turned away northwards, curling back on itself and sliding over the land which is now Caithness. When the glaciers, themselves ephemeral if reckoned against the long drift of time, had passed away, the shore which had carried their enormous weight, as indeed the small cliff on which I now stood, took, as it were, a deep breath and expanded upwards, thus preventing the newly born sea from hurling itself against the rising land.

Looking now across that sea, the Moray Firth, I could pick out small towns strung along the far shore roughly twenty miles away: Lossiemouth with the Covesea Light; Burghead, with its Pictish promontory fort; Kinloss and the RAF a few miles south. At night they were to become strings of bright gold, as if a necklace had been broken up, each short length glittering between dark waters and dark sky and affording me a God's-eye view. By day, it has to be confessed, the heavy shudder of planes, low-flying out of Lossiemouth and Kinloss, made it clear that even on a deserted coast you had inescapably to put up with modern life. And, looking away southward to my right, I could distinguish the harsh lights of the rig-construction base at Ardersier, even now glinting sharply into the soft evening.

The wide stretch of the Moray Firth, as it opened into the North Sea, would prove to be a turbulent and often

unpredictable water, but now it lay gentle and unruffled, a
sheet of soft blue silk shadowed here and there by passing
clouds and seamed by the silver wakes of passing fisher-
boats. I turned my back on the sea and faced the north,
seeing a rolling farmland bounded by the Dornoch Firth
which, together with the Moray, shaped this landscape
into a peninsula. I saw the tall, white, red-ringed lighthouse
at Tarbat Ness, thrusting up between the two firths a mile
or so north of where I stood; saw a sprinkling of farms and
cottages, all beautifully distant from me, though also
promising companionship; saw the long, pale, amethyst
line of the Sutherland hills and the further sheer black
cliffs of Caithness. Yes, it would be solitude, and my heart
rejoiced.

But of course it would be madness even to contemplate
it. Everybody had told me so, again and again, with the
utmost clarity and vigour. Why go so far away? Why leave
everything, every place, every person to which and to
whom you belong? But I had obstinately shaken my head,
well knowing that for me there was never an abiding place
and that, though I might come to this delectable cliff-top in
the far north of Scotland, I might just as easily leave it
again.

That was twelve years ago, and now, with generous care
from kindly landlord friends, and a rent which made
digging up my southern roots possible, the scene is entirely
changed. Today the small house, reconstructed, is light and
airy, a place of many windows and wide horizons, provided
with the basic mod cons and filled with a lifetime's
treasures. The angels, alas, have had to disappear from
view, hidden behind condensation-proof boarding. And
the former lively denizens have long since – and hurriedly –
moved out: those, that is, who managed to escape in time,
assisted by the unremitting attentions of Edward, the
golden, part wild-cat sharer of this retreat. Edward's years of

concern for his own as well as for my welfare were and still are continued expertly, if rather more violently, by Halley, the pugnacious, black-and-white huntress who came to me at the time of the comet. Thus the many fearful scamperings and embattled shrieks, not to mention the alarming gnawings at hidden electricity cables, which echoed so dauntingly in early days from the space between stone wall and giprock board, have become a fading and unregretted memory.

Outside, to the north-west, the quarter-mile farm track brings a varied assortment of vans and trucks, summoned through the telephone's lifeline, to deliver my necessary provisions to the very door (shades of humping heavy shopping baskets up the seventy-eight stairs to a London flat!). The garden, never quite tamed of its wildness, but now kept more or less under control, rolls away in uneven waves of mown grass and low-growing, supposedly gale-resistant plants, into a woodland still offering precarious shelter from feline assault to such birds as choose foolishly to remain. Alas, the many little soft-feathered balls, so still, so seldom to be revived! Goldcrest, firecrest, greenfinch and jenny wren; the rare *Erithacus rubecula rubecula* – our migrant robin; thrush, and lovely, most eloquent blackbird; even a pigeon, left over perhaps from earlier more halcyon days of occupation: all snared by the deviously, enchantingly feminine Halley, whose needle-claws belie other more winning ways, as when she sits upon a wall screwing up her eyes at me in a beguiling, conspiratorial cat-smile.

So I came here, remaining of course that which I had been, an 'incomer', always careful to test my way, even meticulously to forgo my vote at local elections. And what I so happily found has always been warmth and acceptance. Thankfully it has not been my fate to merit that ultimate exclusion of being dubbed a 'white settler'!

There are some very big questions which any of us will ask ourselves when emigrating from one country to another. For it is not so much *Why* have you left? but *What* are you seeking? You who come from another place; you who do not, and cannot quite belong. I suppose my own answer has to be solitude, though never isolation. A time – yes – to keep silence. A place in which to escape the hassle and look around. A chance to learn afresh of the smaller lives, no less important in the scheme of things, of smaller creatures. Not everyone gets the opportunity to do this. Not everyone wants it. But if you do want it, and if you can square your conscience over those needling self-accusations that it would be contracting out of the 'struggle', then, without in any way seeking to become a hermit, and without rejecting any of those things which have always mattered, you may permit yourself to pause awhile; to take, like that raised beach, a long, deep breath. I have, throughout my adult life, held unswervingly to acceptance to two 'commandments'. They are not quite in the style of the greater Ten, but, as the Quakers would put it, they 'speak to my condition'. And the first of these, passionately seen as a guide-line, is W.H. Davies's not always answerable question, 'What is this life. . . .'

In this place, and because of my advanced age, I am able to do just that, and I have come to understand that nothing is ever quite what it seems to be. For this is not a wilderness, though it is wild; not a beauty spot, though beautiful; not a silent place, yet pervaded by quiet; and not isolated, though offering solitude. Total isolation is a suffering, and it can be found in every city, while solitude – the art of being alone – is an altogether different matter, as well as having nothing to do with loneliness.

I cannot lay claim to any morsel of Scottishness, though I enjoy similarly diluted Viking blood from similarly invaded but in my case Norman shores. So there is perhaps a link far back in history. Indeed, there is a rather more recent precedent for my coming here. About 150 years ago, in 1833, a young man of my family, though of a different branch, 'chafed like a caged eagle' at his city life and came to live in his cousin's hunting-lodge of Rosehall in Sutherland. He

then married and moved to Elgin, just across the Moray
Firth from where I am now perched. And there he spent
the last twenty years of his life recording the habits of
Scottish wildlife. His name was Charles St John, well
known as a Scottish naturalist, though coming from the
south, but notorious also for having shot the last osprey of
his day. In his defence (and this is borne out by his vivid
descriptive writings about Scotland's countryside in the
mid-nineteenth century), it has to be said that he was
always much more of an observer than a destroyer of
wildlife. It is a pleasant coincidence that now, as I walk
along 'my' cliff, I can glance across the water and wave my
hand, crying into the wind a gleeful greeting: 'Hallo,
Cousin Charles!' And maybe both of us have been drawn
here by our St John love of wildlife and solitude, surfacing
in many generations. Perhaps the threads go back, even, to
that Normandy sea-coast from which my family had
sprung, Anglicizing themselves after 1066 as St John from
the Saint-Jean they had once been. Certainly the thread is a
tight one between myself and my father, though he was a
man of Devon and never knew the far north. He, like
Charles St John before him, was forced into city living, and
while the London of the early 1900s bore no resemblance to
the frenetic London of today, it became nevertheless a
trap. Thinking back, I see my father as a hermit *manqué*,
whose idea of bliss would have been to live alone in the
middle of Dartmoor. Instead of which, unlike Charles who
was able to break away, his chafing was endless and his
cage lifelong.

   I, in my turn, have also known some city cages. Living in
a high London flat, I would wake in the small hours,
fretfully sensing the persistent glow of artificial light, shed
mercilessly to the horizon and never giving way, as in the
open country, to the necessary dark; aware of tall buildings
crowding me, immobile slabs which could not breathe.
Then I would consider with panic the acres of tarred road
and grey pavement, spread in a thin but effective layer

across the city, a barrier against treading the earth, a giant
prison-yard containing the millions of those resting or
unresting souls. Sometimes I would feel a frantic urge to
hack up the paving-stones and rub a bit of earth between
my fingers. A window-box is no substitute for a small
wood with its drifts of cow-parsley. But, chafing against
my own cages, I succeeded now and then in escaping. These
earlier forays were only partial, could of necessity have
been nothing more. For there was always the 'struggle', in
one form or another, continually and energetically to be
pursued because – as I had found out, suddenly, shockingly,
at a very early age – we are all bound up together, without
exception, brothers and sisters of one another in a world
which did not and does not set much store by such an idea.

But now, on this wild cliff, with the small wood beside
me and the sea below, I can cease for a while to chafe. I am
no eagle, but surely I can shake out my lesser feathers?

— 2 —

When We've Been There Ten Thousand Years

In a farming and fishing community there is little sympathy
for any wildlife that interferes with the business of earning
a living. This is understandable. Easter Ross is a blackspot
of unemployment, any teenager knowing perfectly well
that there is no sense in 'getting on his bike' in pursuit of a
job. It will be gone while he is busy pedalling after it. Those
older men who are safely employed on farms or fishing for
salmon, have read the writing on the wall, and their age-
long enmity against any predator likely to harm their
livestock, and thus their livelihood, is total. Brer Fox,
although I enjoy him as he gracefully leaps through a field
of growing barley, is far from innocent of ravaging new-
born lambs. That roving seal, surfacing from the water
with smooth head and round, appealing eyes, has probably
just bitten a great chunk out of the best part of a salmon.
Or again, perhaps not. No wonder, then, that I used to
meet men along the cliff, watching their nets at sea and
armed with guns, fully determined to take pot-shots at
their rivals. Fortunately a seal's head is exceedingly
difficult to hit as it rises and sinks in a flurry of restless
waves. So it hardly needed my anguished and not entirely
joking cry, 'Over my dead body!', though surprise at my
ridiculous response may have helped spoil their aim!

I comfort myself against the salmon fishers' fierce
denunciations with the rather more informed views of

17

Dr L. Harrison Matthews who, until he died recently, was one of Britain's most distinguished naturalists, especially in the study of the great sea mammals:

> [While] it would not be denied that a seal would be likely to take any fish that it encountered . . . fishermen are very apt to make seals the scapegoats for a scarcity of fish which may very well be due to quite other causes. It should be remembered that seals have been present on our coasts from time immemorial during seasons both of scarcity and abundance of fish.*

It is a nice problem: to balance the need of food for man against the equally important need of food for sea creatures. There is, too, the unfortunate salmon, now so often trapped for life (more accurately, trapped for death) in unhealthy and often poisonous cages. I am not a vegetarian and, even if I were, I should not be entitled to lay down the law for others. But man is a land animal, and it seems to me that he does not have quite the same rights over the sea as do the sea animals. They have chosen to develop their particular skills within the waters of this planet, or, as in the case of dolphins, to return to the oceans after many ages on the land. Also – a decisive point, surely, and among those other causes mentioned by Dr Harrison Matthews – if the waters around our coasts had not been so constantly over-fished, we should not now be man animals struggling with sea animals over what remains.

The present anxiety about the ultimate survival of seals, both the common and the grey, through the threat of rapidly spreading disease, highlights another aspect of the problem. For if our seals die out, whether by disease or by the efforts of that biggest and fiercest of human predators, commercial interests, it will be a further disturbance in the whole chain of balanced creation, as with so many other

---

* *British Mammals* (Collins, 1960).

threatened species, even of the small birds of our demolished hedgerows. Eventually this delicate balance will be thrown irretrievably out of gear. Eventually, we at the top of the pile will have succeeded in undermining ourselves.

Up here, it is thought that the 1988 virus affecting the seal population comes from diseased corpses of sledge dogs, thrown into the sea from Greenland or Iceland. But whatever the precipitating factor in the terrible toll of our northern seals, the origin surely lies in North Sea pollution and the consequent weakening of seal resistance. Apart from the well-known ordinary pollutants, it is only a few years since some packages of nuclear waste slipped off the deck of a ship in trouble in the Moray Firth and plummeted to the bottom of the sea – just across from my cliff-top. We have not heard of their retrieval, or of their condition as they lie, so to speak, 'rocked in the cradle of the deep'.

My first acquaintance with a seal came as I walked along the shore near the lighthouse. I was newly ensconced in the coastguard house, avidly learning its cliff-top way of life and struggling to become familiar with an entirely new set of birds and beasts. Hitherto, although no stranger to small birds and other creatures of the woodland, the larger, wilder occupants of our seashores had been totally unknown to me. I felt almost submerged by the freshness of everything, so taken for granted by those who had long lived here. The birds that wheeled and dived around me were no longer those milder small relations. These were strange, harsh-voiced creatures: herring gulls, black-backs, kittiwakes, violent small terns, all highly competitive; shags and heraldic cormorants; oyster-catchers and fulmars; a glimpse now and then of slow-winging heron, and – mainly dead and washed on to the shore – the pelagic gannet.

Of the land animals, I had not then encountered a wild cat, though agile, half-feral kinsmen would often peer from behind bales of straw in the farm steadings, sharp, pointed little faces frantic with hunger and alarm. But now, as I stood upon that slipway, the water lapping at my feet, I was not thinking of the land. This was an empty and unaccommodating shore. A level stretch of sheep-nibbled turf – that raised beach – ran between the low cliffs and the jumbled, old red sandstone reefs arising from the sea. Far out, an earthquake fissure travelled along the floor of the Moray Firth, the last petering-out of the Great Glen Fault beginning in the far south-west near Oban and Loch Linnhe and streaking up Lochs Lochy and Ness. Even now there are occasional shudders along the Fault, which animals always seem to sense in advance. I remember being surprised and perplexed when a flock of sheep, grazing quietly beyond my windows, began, without any visible cause, pelting frantically from one end of the long cliff-top to the other. Huddling against the whin about a quarter of a mile away, they would then come pounding back until, transfixed by fear, they stumbled to a halt, jammed together and clearly terrified. A few seconds later the process was reversed, the animals bucking and leaping and tearing into each other as they raced back along the narrow track. Less than an hour later there came a small but distinct convulsion rumbling through the ground, and my dustbin, wedged in a corner against the winter gales, was lifted up and tossed away. Various strange objects must have sunk to the bottom of that under-sea ravine, including, so it is said, a First World War battleship. The Fault is the Firth's secret storehouse, well guarded from eager young divers who sometimes arrive here with deep-sea equipment.

The rocks, like all the rocks along this shore, were dark and very ancient, scored by the glaciers into square blocks as if by precision tools and flattened in places into the semblance of a tilted roadway. The sea poured over them, grey-blue in the light of early afternoon. A small, bright-painted boat lay upside-down on a spread of shelly sand. To the left, a mass of sandstone cliff thrust a rampart into the sea. To the right, the grassy shore swung in a great curve to form this sheltering bay. Directly in front, there was nothing much between me and Scandinavia. Then suddenly it was like some magician's trick. One moment the sea was empty; the next, I was looking straight across the water at the hugely rearing figure of a seal. He had surfaced from fishing and was now treading water, unaware of me as yet but alerted, his narrow, smooth, pointed grey head facing out to sea, massive dappled shoulders streaming as the wash of water drained away. He stood upright, immense in dignity. For a moment his muzzle swung slowly to and fro, questing uneasily, and I recalled that seals are said to have the same blurred vision in accommodating from water to air as a human swimmer when below water without goggles. Then, lifting up in magnificent, impassive un-concern, he found me, his dark sorrowing eyes unflinchingly upon me, his shoulders well out of the water, heavy and solid and somehow queerly human.

It was difficult, during those brief, packed moments, lulled by his quiet composure, to register any emotion at all, but I knew – was certain of it – that this was no inferior creature, no lesser being, no sea animal over which to exclaim and be entertained. It was another intelligence, a mind, older and wiser and more profound than I thought I could ever hope to become. We were both equal inhabitants of this world: I, the land-dweller; he, within the seas. We regarded each other formally, and an exchange, seemingly, was made between us, an inner acceptance of each other's not too dissimilar reality.

I held my breath, so close he was, his gentle gaze remaining fixed upon me. He revolved slightly in the frothy eddies, but seeking all the time to keep me within his view. Then slowly, without haste, without fear, he sank beneath the waters. I know I gave a cry – of disappointment and longing. 'But he knew me!' I told myself. 'He recognized me!' It was a confusing idea, but I felt that this recognition was an essential quality between two beings. Not that he was in any way human – no, of course not, simply 'other'.

Rather as if a dweller from outer space, the 'off-worlder' so familiar from science fiction, had come down from some far-away planet in some infinitely distant galaxy, and had brought with him the authority, gentleness and wisdom of a superior civilization, as yet beyond the comprehension of those creatures he now was placed alongside.

'He's gone,' I cried. But he was not gone. The sleek head surfaced once again, this time closer to the shore; the great shoulders rose heavily out of the water, yellow-grey in patches of wet skin, smooth and powerful. I stood very still upon the slipway, consumed by a need to reach out and touch him. I remembered that seals are thought to sing together, and quite suddenly, careless of any astonished watcher, I began those haunting words of the song 'Amazing Grace':

'Through many dangers, toils and snares, we have
already come.
'Twas grace that brought us safe thus far, and grace
will lead us home.'

I sang as clearly as I could across the short few yards of sea dividing us. 'When we've been there ten thousand years, Bright shining as the sun . . .' and he swung with the current, eyes dark and secret. Then slowly, still watching me, he sank again beneath the waters, away and away, with never a ripple to mark his passing. I turned from the shore then, aware that there would not be – need not be – any further affirmation of that bridge across our ten thousand years. A grace had been given between two alien yet allied creatures, and perhaps such grace would one day lead all of us home.

During the following years I often watched the seals. Sometimes they were alone, but usually they were in twos or threes, seen either in that same secluded bay where the fishermen spread out their nets to dry on the sand, or from the top of my own patch of cliff. Never since that first meeting was I close to any of them, but frequently I sat on the edge of the cliff looking down upon them as they rose and sank, rose and sank, questing for food. They would remain only a few moments at the surface, heads uplifted, muzzles pointing to the sky, revolving slowly as they breathed in again after their dive, their small, dark heads hardly distinguishable from the lobster-creel floats. Sinking once more, diving sleekly, they would not go very deep (certainly not more than maybe a hundred feet), since along this kind of coast food is available in relatively shallow water. These were the common seal and, when I timed them as they disappeared, it was about five to seven minutes before they rose again. It is possible for common seals to stay under water for about fifteen minutes without coming up to breathe – some say for a good deal longer – and the grey seals for up to twenty. But an ordinary man, diving, could hold his breath for only about a minute, and even pearl-divers would not be able to remain below much more than two and a half minutes.

The complicated mechanism by which seals can take down sufficient oxygen to last them during a long dive, is a strange miracle. At the moment of descent the seal will blow out most of the air in his lungs in order to reduce buoyancy. But he still contains within his body several reservoirs, or depots, of oxygen. These depots would certainly not last out the average dive if used at surface rate, but, as he dives, the heartbeat drops considerably and blood-flow to the muscles is greatly restricted; also the blood-vessels contract, otherwise the seal would lose consciousness. The slowing of the heartbeat, and consequent conserving of oxygen supply, carries on evenly during the entire dive, however rapidly the seal is moving. And because seals are comparatively insensitive to increased quantities of carbon dioxide, they can endure a long dive without breathing. There is a limit to the time the process will be effective, and woe betide the seals who stay under water longer than they should: if the oxygen content in

their blood falls too low, they will drown. But the
surprising thing is that as soon as they return to the
surface to breathe, the heartbeat is immediately restored
to normal, changing abruptly from ten to 150 a minute. A
human diver, going to a depth of forty-five feet or more,
can suffer from caisson disease, or bends, on surfacing too
swiftly. And seals, also, although they have this intricate
mechanism to protect them, will not be safe should they
dive too steeply and return too rapidly from a great depth.

The automatic sustaining of equilibrium operates invisibly
within the seals' great bodies as they sink and rise. But to the
watcher, as they curve around each other on the surface
of the water, it is as if a group of dancers are performing an
archaic ballet of predetermined movement, effortless, fluid
and infinitely beautiful. The sea around them swells and
ripples; light glances off their dark heads; the pattern of
their individual dance is repeated between them, as it has
been performed and repeated from unknown antiquity.

My garden, one early morning in summer, was speckled
with dew as a light mist rolled out to sea and allowed the
sun to play over the restless small waves. I was near the
edge of the cliff when suddenly I heard a rough bellowing,
the sound of an unhuman wrangle, a fierce disputation
between what seemed to be large animals. It was difficult
to tell where the alarming sounds were coming from, the
mist always altering distances. They might have been just
over the lip of the cliff, and I ran hastily, fearing that Halley
might be in trouble and not knowing in the least what kind
of creature might have attacked her. But when I stood on
the edge of the cliff, peering down and searching among
the whin, there was nothing to be seen. No ferocious
beasts. No mangled puss.

I returned to the garden, only to hear renewed snarls,
certainly from animals growling at and worrying each
other. The noise, which was considerable on that still

morning, now appeared to come from further down the cliff, and again I ran to locate it. This time, as the mist obligingly drifted away, I saw three seals close to the shore and barking furiously. There was a flurry of agitated water until, possibly sensing they were observed, the seals disappeared beneath the surface and made off. But they did not go far, and I could still follow snatches of the argument. So I sat down on the edge of the cliff, wrapped in the quietness of the growing day, and waited.

And then, after a few moments, I heard it – but no longer the quarrelling. That had been mysteriously assuaged, and the sound which now reached me through the fragments of clinging mist was that strange, wonderful, unearthly music, unmistakable and never to be forgotten – so rare as to be almost unbelievable – of seals singing to each other. It came to me with a sense of shock: clear and high and piercingly sweet, a weird, wild music from some lost, forgotten world.

I hardly dared breathe, afraid of what I might miss. But the sound went on and on, thin and cool and unimpassioned, yet also, in some curious way, deeply consoling as it rose and fell in cascades against the listening cliffs. Later I was to find that there had been another watcher on the shore that morning, he too hardly daring to believe what he was hearing.

But at last the enchantment was over, and the world settled back into place. The sea lay placid now, and the growing light played over the newly warmed rocks. The seals had taken themselves away, that incredible purity of sound withdrawn. I sat there for a long time, dazed, but giving thanks for what I had been privileged to hear. A flute would be, perhaps, the closest counterpart to such music, yet a flute would sound warmly human beside those incorruptible, unearthly voices.

3

'A Very Competent Cat'

Edward came into my life in the spring of 1979. His age was uncertain, but probably he was about six years old. He had been dumped in the village, two miles away, most likely from a car by people who could no longer be bothered with him, and was then passed around, after living rough for some time, from one family to another, settling nowhere and wanted by none. Rather naturally he ended up a 'damaged' cat, manifesting the same fears and insecurity an unwanted human being would have shown: afraid of people and wary of attachment. I had had my doubts whether he would settle with me, but in that moment when he was lifted from the cat-crate and placed on the carpet by the fire, he simply rolled over on his back and gently, gracefully, waved his paws in the air. He had come home.

Edward was a heavy, golden-orange, softly striped cat, with a larger than usual backbone which seemed not quite to fit into the rest of his bone structure. Something had gone agley in the genetic union of his parents, so that, together with his thick, ringed tail, he might well have sprung from the mating of wild cat with feral cat. His short, plush fur which, unlike the later Halley, he adored having brushed, his white shirt-front, his green-gold eyes, made him an altogether splendid creature, and, after his advent, there followed six and a half years of mutual devotion. And since this is as honest a chronicle as I can devise, I must risk the accusation of mawkishness and say that indeed he became for me the child I had never had. So that when he became old and ill and in loving kindness had to be set free, I nursed him day and night, getting up at his every cry, to assist him back to his bed in the armchair near the fire, or to wrap him warmly in his woolly blanket.

But first there were those splendid years when Edward, in his full glory, became known far and wide, his photograph going out on home-made Christmas cards to Edward lovers as far afield as Alaska and Germany, Canada and Israel. One of his admirers, regarding his 1982 portrait, said of him reflectively: 'What a very *competent* cat!' And this he certainly was. A hunter, yes, though he found birds – to my infinite relief – just boring. Perhaps he disliked the scratchiness of a mouthful of feathers.

The coastguard house was by then home for me as well as Edward. The rats had departed, the replacement mice were very quickly eliminated by Edward, and it seemed that all things were indeed bright and beautiful. Indeed, as I looked out one morning, I should have said that surely there could be little that was more beautiful than the creature poised so elegantly upon a rock beyond the window. Within the garden, the place having been a coastguard station, there were several stone compounds, now used for vegetables, and some broken-up lengths of wall which I had made into rockeries, trailing down the grass towards the edge of the cliff. Here, winding among tiny tunnels and between heaped-up stones, ran the main thoroughfares, the highways and byways of the local stoat family. For the polished little creature I now beheld – rich chestnut fur, white front, inquisitive small head and bright, intelligent eyes – was undoubtedly a male stoat. I could even see the black tip to his thin tail, distinguishing him from the lesser weasel.

In that moment, as he sat bolt upright, thin paws raised prayerfully, sniffing the air for any hint of danger, I rejoiced in him. And when eventually he dropped to all four paws, not running but seeming to flow away between the

stones and into the recesses of the rocks, appearing and
disappearing every few seconds, alert and groomed and
with his swashbuckling air of bravado, I gave thanks that I
had seen this wonderful piece of creation – beautiful, eager,
aware, and deadly. Yes indeed, a precision instrument for
killing, one of the few creatures that dealt out death for the
sheer joy of destruction, thereby rivalling, but never
equalling, man.

But in those first moments, and in the days that
followed, I did not dwell upon the lethal possibilities. I saw
only grace and beauty, dazzled by those brilliant, perceptive
eyes. And even when later he or one of his relations was
seen from the window moving silently and sinuously along
the paving outside the back door, snuffling with insatiable
curiosity at the framework, it never occurred to me that
perhaps, just perhaps, the whole family had once assumed
that my fine new home had rightfully belonged to them. I
should have remembered the pigeon droppings, those
holes in the floor, the empty window-frames.

The house was not exactly a house, being a one-storey
building, and my bedroom was therefore at ground level,
so that I could lie in bed and look out at the sea through that
glass-paned back door which led directly into the garden.
Well, it was summer, and all the doors and all the windows
were open to the sun. Anybody could walk in. And, as it
turned out, somebody did.

Summer up here means that the sun will set towards the
north not long before eleven o'clock, but it was fully dusk
that night when I went to bed, and the whole cliff-top was a
place of shadows. I slept alone, meaning that Edward was
barred. Not for me a cosy cat upon my eiderdown, though
perhaps it would have been more far-sighted of me to have
included his company. As it was, I had scarcely edged my
way down the bed when, from behind the pillows, there
came an explosion of chattering fury as my reconnoitring
stoat bounced into view just inches from my nose. He was
raging, utterly unafraid and bent on havoc. After all, the

only part of my anatomy to be considered was a head upon the pillow. Even an intelligent stoat had no means of knowing that there was a larger extension of body attached. But the head did not remain submissively quiescent and, as I reared up, screaming wildly, there was a flick of darkness and the intruder vanished. Yes of course I screamed. Who wouldn't have? Not that it was any help, even had the attacker been human and therefore that much more determined. There was nobody along that stretch of solitary cliff to hear my shrieks. And anyway it might have been a sheep, or even a distressed seagull.

The stoat, rather naturally, had taken refuge behind some furniture, and though I proceeded to take the place apart, aided with great interest by the hastily awakened Edward, I knew I could never hope to catch up with it. Had I not already learnt from my 'cousin' Charles that when a stoat is really moving, few dogs even can overtake it? Flowing like water, it would outpace any efforts of mine, while Edward had no chance to manoeuvre in this very small room. So I opened the door to the outer world and convinced myself, after several hours had slipped by, that my visitor had departed. What was left of the night passed uneasily, but certainly I had at last acquainted myself with the smell of stoat.

They say that lightning never strikes twice in the same place. So, for a whole week, I went to bed and gently to sleep without giving the matter another thought. But then came the night when, pushing my feet down to the bottom of the bed and settling my head comfortably into the pillows, I became suddenly aware of a convulsion *within* the bed, around my feet. Not, I was glad to note, actually between the sheets but only a layer of blanket removed from where I lay. And then, most unpleasantly, came a rippling wave of movement as the stoat (could it be anything else?) shot up the length of my body, to emerge, gibbering with rage, upon my pillow and, once again, inches from my nose. But it did not go. It sat there for

several seconds, an eternity, no doubt trembling as much
as I was, and uttered its harsh, throaty curses – compounded
probably as much of fear as defiance. Once again I
screamed, leaping from those constricting blankets. Once
again the creature poured away, disappearing decently
behind a curtain. Once again I obediently opened the door
to point the way out.

But I could sympathize with him. The place, so far as he
was concerned, had been changed beyond recognition. No
pigeons for supper. No convenient holes in the floor. My
sympathy did not, however, make me any more eager to
share my home. Indeed, such was my fear for that small
piece of face which would lie temptingly upon the pillow in
sleep – especially for that beak-like St John nose, always my
bane and now a most obvious target – that for several
nights I slept with an aluminium colander carefully
arranged across my vulnerable features. I told myself that
it was hardly different from a medieval knight's helmet and
that I could at any rate breathe through the holes.

Eventually it was Edward who settled the affair. Summing
up the situation, he moved slowly but powerfully into
action.

A few mornings later I went out into the garden. It was
one of those dew-on-the-grass days, the lawns glittering as
brightly as the sea beyond. The sun, already high, lit up the
whole of my world, each shoot and leaf and bud delicately
picked out in greenness, the darker pine trees of my wood
standing quietly in the background. There was a wall, part
of the compound of the coastguard look-out post. And on it
sat Edward. Nothing particularly strange about that, only
there was something in the way he held himself, so
upright, with an air of modest pride, that told me he wished
to draw attention to himself. So I walked across, looking up
at him. He seemed just the same as usual, but then I saw
one small alteration. On his pink nose was a single drop of
blood. And yes, there was a smell. Quickly stepping back, I
almost fell over the very dead stoat which lay at my – and

his – feet, the back of its neck neatly broken. Edward did not move a muscle, gave not a flicker of self-congratulation. He smugly went on sitting in a peculiarly haughty fashion, staring out across the corpse of his victim but utterly ignoring it.

There was a sequel in which, having to dispose of the body, I also took the smell upon me, and both Edward and I had to retire to the kitchen sink where I rubbed and scrubbed him, endlessly, all over, to do away with that most noxious and peculiar of scents.

It was only a few days later that I came upon Edward as he disappeared up the chimney in pursuit of a weasel. Grabbing him frantically by the back legs before he got irrevocably stuck, I hauled him down again. He descended in a rush of soot that settled stickily upon us both.

After this there was a final occasion when, looking from a window, I saw a large rabbit fleeing across the lawn. It was pursued hotly by a stoat, which in turn was pursued, also hotly, by Edward. Anxious to do my bit, I joined the cavalcade. The stoat at once dived for cover. Edward cleverly blocked its get-away, while I, dithering, eventually assisted at the obsequies. The rabbit, meanwhile, had disappeared discreetly over the horizon.

In all, Edward disposed of five stoats and four weasels, though not always escaping unscathed. Disheartened, the remaining families packed up and moved down the cliff to join relations living rather more peacefully on the shore.

Yes, a very competent cat.

And I was grateful. But, red in tooth and claw? Certainly I was, as much as Edward, and both of us equally with the stoat. We did not, any of us, indulge in that 'I – Thou' relationship where 'all real living is meeting'. Yet Edward was innocent of bad intent, and the stoat also; their actions were never carried out with malice aforethought. Nor were they – nor could they be – conscious of sin. The

enigma faces me daily, for however comfortably I may live
among my cliff-top wildlife, I cannot remain unaware of
the many small deaths and the blind terror of the hunted,
not always caused by man, but certainly the darker side of
the way we relate to the animal creation.

I walk along the cliff, rejoicing in the wind, the light and
colour, the tumbled shore, the honey-smelling whin, the
far blue hills, but then I come upon herring gulls wrangling
over the not-quite corpse of an erstwhile companion; he,
for some reason, weaker than they and therefore to be
eliminated. I turn the corner of the house on a new and
fresh-washed morning, the corn springing green beyond
the garden fence, and encounter a roe-deer, turned to
stone and warily surveying me as I too try to make myself
invisible. He bears the confrontation for a few moments,
but alas he understands the dark all too well and is taking
no chances. So he flashes away in splendid, graceful leaps.
Just in case. I walk in my wood, that sanctuary as I had
hoped, and come upon a small pile of bright green feathers.
I had watched it earlier, from the kitchen window, as it
flickered lightly through the twisted branches.

There is always a darkness conjured up when we allow
an unnecessary killing. This is true whether of man or
beast, and I believe that the Creator does not distance
himself from the smaller tragedies, but that they are
included within his own being, the dignity of every
creature being important to him. We have learnt, often
glibly, that not a sparrow falls to the ground but the Lord
knows about it, and this seems rather clever of him and
supports his omnipresence. But we rarely imagine that it is
a piece of himself that is being hurt.

The belief in a God who suffers continually within his
whole creation is one of the Christian heresies I have
consistently held, even though I have rejected many pieces
of doctrine considered by some to be utterly necessary. I
accept that he contains within himself all darkness as well
as light. This must be so or, for me, he is not God. The dark

of our world seems mainly to arise out of our wrong choices: often such woeful choices that a case could be, and has been, made out for so-called 'natural' disasters being indiscriminate rebellions of the very earth we abuse. Possibly, in some far-off reaches of the universe, other created beings may have made better choices. Meanwhile we have our own problem with the 'evil inclination' resulting from that ancient and symbolic catastrophe we have thought of as the Fall.

There is a story from Jewish mysticism which for me enlarges and interprets my own gropings. It tells that when God began his act of creation, he broke off a piece of himself to form the universe and everything that is in it. When it all went wrong, as it so observably did and is still doing, God suffered within the suffering, and is still suffering. Therefore, it is argued, it is not so much a question of God's helping us, but of our suffering with him in the act of restoration. The Jewish faith, being essentially optimistic, thus holds out the eventual expectation of a healed, or whole, creation.

All this, then, on account of a very beautiful and very lethal small animal, killed, together with several members of his family, by a somewhat larger and, as it happened, rather more lethal 'enemy'. Not to mention the one who stood aside, rejecting active participation but doing nothing to prevent what happened – openly grateful to the killer who did the job for her. In such ways, with many excuses, and in many different situations, do we keep our hands clean. But, as a 1960s ballad succinctly put it, 'We are all sat down in one boat together', and there are no easy answers as to which bit of creation occupies the Creator's most earnest attention. Maybe he did not entirely approve of his son sending those devils into a herd of peaceful swine?

4

Gulley

My cliff-top life can be neatly divided into two distinct
historical periods, according to the two cats who have
permitted me to look after them: the Edwardian age,
during which the golden Edward kept the place – and me –
in order, and the Halleysian one, when that black-and-
white and extravagantly feminine creature turned everything upside-down, pursuing her own entirely selfish aims
and wasting no time at all upon house protection. Both
enjoyed going with me for scrambles up and down the
cliffs, but whereas Edward faithfully plod every step of
the way, plunging among the whin as we scaled trackless
heights, Halley would dart along just as far as she chose
and not an inch beyond, vanishing as if by magic among
rocks and scrub in pursuit of suddenly discovered prey, and
arriving back at the house hours later. Well, she is a
huntress, and as such leads a double life, demanding her
cat-food comfort beside a warm fire but never losing sight
of her one and only real interest: those small creatures laid
regularly at my feet as if to instruct me that thus and thus
might I, too, successfully catch my dinner. Her anxiety to
impress this lesson upon me is obvious, as is her exasper-
ation at my stupidity, my inability to learn. So I clear away
what is left of the little corpses, and have learnt at least one
lesson: that our standards are different, and that she – a cat
with a cat's instincts – must not be branded with our
conscious, human cruelties. If I grieve over her many
captives, she will simply sit upon the doorstep, meticulously

washing her paws and giving me sidelong glances of incredulity.

It was during Halley's reign that an unlikely and highly complicated event occurred which engulfed us both for weeks and even led on her part to a short, sharp nervous breakdown.

Gulley arrived on the lawn one afternoon of early summer. He was a herring gull, still mottled and streaked with the dusky brown plumage of the immature bird. It would be three years before he achieved the pale, strong shape of an adult, moving like a snowflake along the winds. But at this first meeting I doubted whether he had even three weeks, since his left wing primaries were broken and bent, trailing on the ground so that he could not fly. It was clear that even if the wing were eventually to knit together, he might, long before then, attract the attention of adult gulls who would briskly tear him to pieces.

I watched him as he humped his way, flat-footed and slow, across the grass, pecking here and there at a few grubs. I wondered, with a growing sense of helplessness, why he had chosen just this place to settle into, for clearly he had decided to do so. Then, looking about me, I realized that, from a gull's-eye view, the grass along the cliff rose at least to a yard high, ungrazed as yet by the usual sheep, and that the fields for miles around were thick with wheat. It was no place for a damaged sea-gull trailing his wing. In fact my garden was the one cropped island in a tall, green-growing ocean. I could see his point. So I stood there, brooding over what to do and noting that Halley sat upon a nearby wall, her gaze riveted by the splendid meal before her. I sighed.

Yet she did not attack, and I remembered that cats will not even pick up a cornered mouse providing it stays quite still, though one flick of movement and all would be over. The young gull appeared quite incapable of any such hasty action, and his slow, unruffled progress seemed only to mesmerize Halley. Perhaps, too, she saw that, young as he was, his size was considerable, and his savage grey beak a disconcerting weapon. I approached him cautiously, and he sidled away, regarding me suspiciously but without alarm. His cold eyes were empty of either fear or supplication. I thought he was as vicious a bird as were the rest of his beautiful, screaming, belligerent tribe. I also thought that he was injured and helpless, and deserved a chance.

But what chance? During the next few days I was bombarded with good advice. Ring the vet and have him put out of his misery (but he wasn't miserable). Ring the RSPB and let them take him away (but he seemed to prefer the garden). Leave him alone, don't fuss him. If he lives, he lives; if not, then not. This from a visiting bird expert, fitting perfectly my own reluctant resolution. After all, Gulley seemed to have chosen this garden, and if eventually he had to die, it was a peaceful spot in which to do it. Or it would be if I could keep Halley away from him. Anyway, I did not see why he should be subjected to the panic of capture and upsetting attention.

So we both, Halley and I, began a period of adjustment to our most unwelcome visitor. It was no time at all before he began, like the greylag geese with Konrad Lorenz, to see me as his mother substitute, hustling across the lawn when I emerged in the early morning, drooping around as I hung the washing on the line, avidly drawing near as I tossed him chunks of cat-meat. Mercifully he omitted that ultimate signal of dependence, which I saw so often as I watched the shore-nesting gulls bring up their young: that mopping and mowing of the infant bird as it begs for the parent's regurgitation of a tasty morsel.

It was several days before the penny dropped and I realized that the garden provided no water. After some searching, I found an old, deep, wooden drawer, lined it with a sheet of plastic and laid it on the grass in a sheltered corner where his splashings would not alert any predatory relations. I filled it with buckets and buckets of water, from then on a daily task, and awaited results. Gulley was delighted. Once the awkward side of the drawer was clambered over, he would wallow to his heart's content, slopping to and fro and flapping his undamaged wing, while he pecked up any small, escaping wildlife disinclined to take a bath.

Halley was in torment. Still wary of approach, she had spent several days stalking him from behind bushes. His lack of fluttering, rapid movement, as he waddled quietly around the garden, seemed to embarrass her: instinct said attack, but as yet there was no precise provocation to trigger the impulse. Also, there was that cruel beak. But after a week or so, disgusted to find him popping up everywhere in her own territory, Halley lost her head and began taking little runs at him, shooting across the lawn, then sheering off at the last moment and doing a kind of bouncing act. Gulley would squawk indignantly and wave his good wing. And Halley, affronted, would retire to a wall or a garden seat or a window-sill – any vantage-point which raised her safely, and importantly, above her enemy. She had most certainly experienced the swooping gulls along the cliff and was not at all sure how far she might rely upon Gulley's invalid condition.

There were thousands of herring gulls nesting, feeding and bringing up their young on the stretch of cliff which bordered my shore. Over the years they had infiltrated steadily along this coast, even driving out the fulmars – those lovely, quiet, dark-eyed, pelagic gliders who breed upon the cliff but then return, as other petrels, to the sea. One of my summer's pleasures is to sit on the edge of the cliff watching two or three fulmars as they sheer and bank and glide, rigid like small aircraft and with tails fanned wide, up and down, up and down, along the whole length of cliff, their thick necks and narrow wings distinguishing them at once from any gull. Unlike the gulls, they tend not to 'follow the plough', sweeping constantly and elegantly along the cliff-face and out to sea, where they live mostly on fish, molluscs and sometimes dead birds. Their nests, each containing the one white egg, are lodged in crevices of the cliffs, alongside the encroaching gulls. They are an obvious minority, living with the inconspicuous secretness of many human minorities, in the midst of yet separated from the racist majority. It is not the fulmar that a smallish black-and-white cat need be afraid of, but the large, combative herring gull or, worse still, the even larger and more bloodthirsty great black-backed gull – that sweeping, jet-winged, harsh-crying, magnificent creature, quite capable, I have often anxiously thought, of picking up a frightened cat and dropping it somewhere out on the far rocks at sea.

So it was no wonder that Halley's approach to this deeply resented incomer was circumspect. And over the weeks that followed, it seemed that the conflict in her between exercising caution and the urge to kill any feathered object became almost unendurable. Halley grew excited and irritable and wild, her easily aroused jealousy swinging her between extravagant demands for a loving lap and sudden spite and needle-claws. It was all very human.

Over the weeks Gulley's wing began to heal, though at first this process was hardly perceptible. He stumped around the garden or sat blissfully in his swimming-pool, or dozed rashly on the lawn with head turned back among his feathers. And he pursued me relentlessly every time I poked my head out of the house. Then, one bright evening about a month later, Gulley flapped both wings and did a little jig. Up and down he jumped, both feet together, up and down and almost airborne. It was too much for Halley. Here was what she had been waiting for: the flurry and flutter of a luscious meal. She flew across the lawn and hurled herself at him. There was a furious agitation of feathers and fur, a cascade of squawking and, surprisingly, Gulley appeared at least six yards away, having neatly taken off. He left behind him a disconcerted Halley, glaring balefully. But he had at last found out how to fly. It took a hunting cat to teach him.

After this there was no holding Gulley. He hopped and flapped and dithered and danced, each day notching up fresh records, as when he managed the vegetable garden wall – sacred to Halley, who did not rest until she had driven him along it to the very end. There were precarious landings, once in an enveloping bush of cotton lavender. But steadily, day by day, he became more proficient until at last he scaled his Everest – perched triumphantly upon the central roof-ridge of the house. From that splendid peak he was able to extend his flights in all directions, flapping, slow-winged, across the wheat-fields and over the cliffs. I watched with trepidation as he joined other gulls riding the air currents, but by now he was so large and clearly powerful that they ignored him.

It was then that one of the most magical moments of this strange experience took place. I had walked as usual down the farm track to pick up the milk, regularly left at the bottom. Turning, I began the quarter-mile ascent to the house. I could see Gulley perched far away on the roof-ridge, but suddenly he took off, swooping fast down the track to meet me, and then escorting me back in long loops of flight, out across the wheat and around my head as I plodded along. He was, I knew, staking his claim, and, while realizing that this could not – must not – be allowed to happen, I felt overwhelmed with surprise and joy that this completely wild creature could recognize and accept me. He swept in low circles about me, skimming the tops of the wheat on either side of the track, his wing-beats steady, keeping me always in his sight. And as I stopped and gazed upward and saluted him, I understood with amazement that, strange and violent and utterly unhuman though he was, we had in some miraculous manner communicated with each other. There had been a meeting between us, a thread of awareness operating at some deeper level than that of his own savage nature or of my complicated humanity. We returned up the track together, and all the while he guarded me with the sweep of his wings.

It was then that I knew I must restore Gulley to his own kind. Nor for me the 'gull in my garden' syndrome. He belonged to the wild, and wild he should remain, never to be humanized, never to become degraded into a cosy conversation piece. He was to be free like other gulls, somehow or other taken back among them. I decided to go for regular walks along the cliff, hoping that he would follow and be drawn by the other gulls to their cliff dwellings. He took to these walks with the utmost energy, released from the constrictions of a planted garden and circling above me as he practised his newly won flying skills. Once I missed him, and found that he had alighted on a rock buttress housing a family of gulls with two or three young. I hid behind the whin, and presently saw how Gulley sidled up to one of the older birds and patiently, pathetically, began the mopping and mowing ritual of a young offspring towards his parent. Alas, it met with no response. Not mine, they seemed to say firmly, and turned their backs on him. But I noticed that they did not attack or even drive him off. It was perhaps his crucial moment of readmission to the tribe. He was not yet welcome, but not cast out. I hastily went back to the house, hoping that Gulley would now remain on the cliff. This, I soon realized, was too much to expect. For when I looked out later, there he was, settled comfortably on a wall as if the place belonged to him.

But it was a beginning, and as his flight powers increased, so did his journeys, until once again it was Halley who organized a second and final break. Gulley was perched one evening upon a wall, staring at the setting sun, when Halley sprang at him from behind, sailing up the back of the wall in one wild rush of outrage. As it happened, I was watching and had my camera with me, so I was able to capture that near-tragedy: Halley appearing beside him like a venomous black and silver demon, and – only just in time – the convulsive lurch as Gulley leapt into the air and took off. It was indeed a close-run thing, and apparently it taught Gulley a lesson. He left at once, beating off across the fields. But of course he eventually came back – kept on coming back – and I then began the sad process of weaning him. First, I withdrew his food (Halley's cat-meat!), knowing that now at last he was able to fend for himself. Then I removed the bathing-pool. And for a few days, whenever I spotted his approach, I hastened indoors, shutting myself away until he had gone.

It was a miserable time, though not of course for Halley, who began to feel the garden once again belonged to her and rapidly recovered from her nervous breakdown. I saw Gulley infrequently, sometimes standing around on the lawn, just waiting, or perched disconsolately on the roof-ridge. But increasingly his visits became shorter as he began to fly along the cliff and out over the sea with other gulls. In the beginning I could often single him out, something perhaps just a bit awkward in the use of his wing, something separate in his behaviour among the vast, spreading clouds of gulls as they breasted the wind, ever watchful for a shoal of fish. Later it became more difficult. Sometimes I would see him, sweeping up the skies and riding the quick-moving air, exulting in the range and power of his wings. Sometimes I would just think I could see him, telling myself that *there* he was, rising and falling and floating until he became a small, dark speck far above my head, expert now in handling the pull and push of our easterly winds. After some months I still imagine that it must be Gulley who suddenly is flying so low across the garden. But he does not touch down. And I can never be sure.

In writing about Gulley, as about the seal, I have stressed that strange, underlying unity (of spirit, nature, of living 'stuff'?) which occasionally makes its presence known between human and animal. But I think it should not be over-emphasized. You do not and cannot converse with a seal. You do not and cannot communicate in human terms with a sea-gull. That there exists some often magically satisfying thread between you both, is undeniable. So you give thanks for its fleeting, flashing manifestation, while knowing that it is but a momentary spark of recognition, which may not be pursued or grasped at.

When I look back, I can see that there has been only one single experience in my life in which my own communication with a non-human creature has approached verbalized emotion – and certainly it was the emotion that was apprehended and not the words. It happened long before I came to Scotland, when I was living in Suffolk and observed one morning a thrusting, vehement trail of grass divots being thrown up by moles across a newly made patch of lawn. I watched with shocked and horrified anguish as my handiwork was ruined, lumps of earth flying out in straight lines as a double tunnel bored through the soil beneath. In that moment I forgot everything. Forgot I was human. Forgot they were moles. I just stood there, stricken, and cried aloud to them in desperate appeal: 'Oh no! Please, *no!* Oh, please, PLEASE, *go away!* Go *away!* Oh, please!'

They went at once. And they never came back. This may sound improbable, but it happened. In that despairing cry – totally unconscious as I was of any distinction between myself and the moles – there must have been some current of communication, direct and unhindered, which mysteriously affected what was going on below ground. From the moment I spoke, everything ceased, the frantic lines of unheaval and destruction stilled, cut short even as I made my plea. Destruction? Yes, but only from my own point of view. The moles were merely building themselves a comfortable extension. Yet they went. And they never came back. I cannot explain it. I can only say it happened.

Thinking and talking about it, as I have done so many times, I feel certain that I could have reached them only *because* of my own complete unconsciousness of what I was doing. I acted spontaneously, discarding the separateness of my own human condition. I appealed to them with that same lack of self-awareness as when I would sometimes turn back to apologize if I had accidentally trodden on a plant or bumped into one. Plants had never noticeably responded to my hasty 'Oh, I'm *sorry!*' How should they? But the moles could, and did. Later I discovered that I could not communicate ever again in that way, simply because I had become self-conscious, and communication requires an absolute unawareness of any barriers. Perhaps this quandary is somehow akin to the unawareness of mankind in that earlier Garden which, exchanged for awareness, severed the natural bonds between all creation and drove out those who sought to become individual. For now the barriers are fixed. But we can still, if we wish, look over the top and recognize each other.

5

The Fall of Icarus

The coastguard house stands high above the rolling farmland. Properly speaking, it turns its back upon the sea, its front door facing north-west down the rough track which leads off the narrow road between the village and the lighthouse. Whichever way you choose to look, from south of Ben Wyvis, our nearest mountain, to the distant Morven peering between far northern summits, a long line of delectable hills unfolds across the horizon. True weather indicators, they can be sharp-edged and almost navy blue with an imminent threat of rain. Or they can offer the first thin coating of snow along their autumn ridges, warning of what is to come when the snow creeps down to meet the water. Or they may just lie there, half asleep, pale hyacinth and dusted with a light mist, the promise of a golden day. But, equally, they may simply not be present. No hills, no sea, only the soft white Scottish *haar* rolling across the land and blotting it out.

During winter snowfalls it is fascinating to see how a complete and self-contained 'storm', round and white like an enormous ball, will detach itself from those hills, twenty miles away as the crow flies, and come bowling along over land and sea in one great compact mass. Alongside it, perhaps some miles distant, may be another giant white cloud, pursuing its own entirely separate path. You watch them approach, seeming so soft and woolly, until in a matter of seconds one of them arrives, and instead of a fluffy plaything your surroundings are wiped out in a tearing, horizontal stream of piercing snow. No soft, slow flakes falling casually out of the winter sky, but a relentless demon-driven onslaught. Within only a few more moments the whole great heavenly snowball has swept over the cliff and out to sea, sometimes losing itself within the water but often retaining its shape above the surface. You find that you have been blown around 180 degrees, so that you may conveniently watch it, still cohering within itself and now apparently just that same woolly snowball, bearing down at speed upon the far Moray shore.

But it was one of the golden days, with the RAF thundering up the Dornoch Firth on bombing practice, that drew me suddenly to the window. Had there been an explosion, or was it just the trailing, seconds-after roar of planes tracking in towards their target? The Firth itself was out of sight behind the opposite swell of farmland, and at first nothing seemed amiss. But as I looked out, I saw the column of smoke rising into the summer sky, saw the heavy, broken fragments of metal plunging towards the Firth, saw the tails of two planes dropping fast. And then, with relief, distinguished the four tiny grey specks, arrested in their fall as the parachutes bloomed hugely above their heads. I watched with fearful anxiety, straining to know whether they would be safe – as indeed it turned out to be, for they fell into the waters of the Firth and were picked up immediately by fishing-boats. But their descent was slow, and they fell as wind-blown seeds. Taking my binoculars off them for a second, I noticed, at the bottom of my track, a group of men and tractors, the men chatting together before going off for their 11.30 meal. I knew them all, and could tell that in the clatter of machines none of them had heard what was happening. Also, from where they were standing, they would not see those falling bits of thistledown. And with surprise I remembered the Brueghel picture of the fall of Icarus, where the ploughman continued undisturbed in his plodding labour and the shepherd gazed tranquilly at nothing, and behind them both the two legs of Icarus scarcely caused a ripple as he disappeared beneath the water. What I was now seeing was a re-enactment of that picture, a modern version of a scene painted three hundred years ago. The tragedy, the plunge from heaven to earth, unseen, unheeded by those whose sights were still, today, fixed upon other ways of living.

One of the strange things about my quiet days up here has been the way in which certain incidents, happening now, have the power to bring back to me other happenings from out of a long-distant past. I find myself beginning to piece together those events, now conjured into abrupt new life, and evidently, whether or not I realized it at the time, holding for me a profound significance. The fall of Icarus, played out that summer day in Scotland, was matched in my mind with my worst memory of the 1914–1918 war. At the time I was scarcely seven years old, cocooned in the safe world of childhood, out of which I was to be shocked into a horrified maturity. It happened during an early period of the war when Zeppelin raids were prominent – always deeply feared by people living near London, possibly because there was something stealthy and unnatural about those vast, unrelenting shapes: enormous creatures of fantasy, sluggishly and with seeming mindlessness nosing out all that was vulnerable and destroying it.

On that particular night I had been put to bed long before the warning came, knowing nothing of my parents' anxiety. I had said good-night to my room, chatting placatingly towards the shadowy recess where something nameless might be lurking, and hoping it would appreciate that I was still quite young and not of any consequence. I had enjoyed, in the fading light, the criss-cross lattice-work of my flowered wallpaper, within the patterning of which my discerning eyes had long since discovered a secondary secret population of shapes and figures, repeated endlessly as the flowers themselves were repeated, and making up yet another world within a world for my private consideration. And I had slept right through into the night when my parents roused me, sodden with sleep and confused by the strangeness of what was happening. I remember being wrapped in a blanket and carried, shoulder-high, into the road outside, which for some reason promised a larger measure of safety than the house itself. It was very quiet, a brooding hush broken only by the whispers of shadowy figures pacing uneasily up and down.

The 'village' in which we lived was no true village, being but an imitation of an 'olde worlde' hamlet, built on the outskirts of the city. The villagers, indeed, were all business people like my father, who went to London every day. Never in any sense a community, they now drew protectively together. Reassuring little messages passed between us all; short bursts of laughter, too high-pitched for mirth, spurted out and were instantly suppressed as if the Zeppelin might hear us when it drifted over. It all took a long time. Sometimes I trotted beside my parents, clutching my blanket round me; sometimes I thankfully accepted the shelter of my father's arms. The night was very dark, though livened incessantly by the sweeping beams of searchlights, fingers which probed and sought and lingered and never gave up.

When at last it came, it slipped past us quietly, a fleeting shadow against the night, a huge greyhound of the skies heading north over a dark city. Somehow we always knew that we had felt its breath, though it must have been miles away. Once gone, it seemed there was nothing left to do. We noted the switch of searchlights. We stood around in small groups, low-voiced, glad to be together. And suddenly, when our backs were turned from the north, when the white streamers of the searchlights seemed wearyingly ineffectual – suddenly, we knew that they had caught it, and the guns began their destruction.

It was far from us now, hovering over Potters Bar, when a flaming shower of crimson fire poured down the sky and brought us, running, on to the vantage-point of the village green. My father had picked me up, jammed against the crowd. And there it was, hanging in the north, black silhouette against the flames which were convulsing it. It took but a few moments until, with an awful finality, the whole great shape broke slowly apart across the middle, two blackened halves, plunging earthward through scarlet fire, the tiny gondola detached and sharply silhouetted, and – ultimate horror – little black specks of human life dropping without hope, without mercy, through the holocaust.

It was in that dreadful moment, when my mind clicked sharply into a total comprehension of what was happening, when my seven-year-old being gasped with the shock of it and the fearful awareness of what those little black sticks were doing, that I heard the sound: the deep, long, animal roar of the crowd; the guttural exultation lifting as one inhuman voice towards that rose-red sky; the mindless savagery belling from one united throat. Child though I was, I recognized that ancient cry, dredged out of some primitive core of being. I clung, sickened, to my father, while he, like my mother, was mercifully silent.

The sound went with me, walked beside me, year in, year out. And though I could not, at seven, have formulated the thought, I knew in my bones even then that the grey hunter, ruthless in victory as it would have been, contained my doomed and necessary brothers.

That intimation of our fragile and precarious mortality, that evocation of the satisfied animal within us, was perhaps the starting-point of a whole series of crucial experiences, leading me, over the years, towards passionately held convictions from which issued my own particular way of life. On the whole it was an unwavering way, even if so frequently pursued in the face of exasperated disapproval. The roots of all I have been during a long life lie far back in that moment of childhood when I refused to identify with the herd.

The Great War ended, so far as my parents and I were concerned, with an enormous bonfire on the village green, an event I was unable to enjoy, since, lurking behind my eyelids were those little black sticks floating down the orange sky, so remarkably like the crackling twigs around which the village celebrated. I remember instead devoting myself to the less hungry beauty of sparklers, then and for ever the firework which most entranced me. We stuck them in the grass around the pond, where they bloomed into starry flowers. And the little black sticks and the mindless voices were carefully covered up and hidden away. I never spoke about them, and since I was anyway a silent child, occupied with my own inner world, it probably did not seem as if anything disturbing had happened to me.

In those days I had not heard of Icarus, let alone of his inventive parent. The boy who, emulating the father, flew disastrously into the sun, only to fall to earth, would certainly have terrified me. Leave it alone, I would have advised. Don't interfere. Stay where you are. Only then can you be safe. So when, as I grew up, I found myself doing exactly the opposite and jumping right in to ask those awkward rash, questions of 'Why?' and 'Where?' and 'Who?' I often discovered that my interferences were scorching my own wings, impelled from within to actions which must be undertaken, but which caused me anguish to enter upon.

The legendary Icarus is a singularly muddled myth. We do not know what, if anything, it cost him to dare such an adventure. Was it simply out of a sense of filial duty? Or was it the child's desire to out-fly the father? Or could it have been only a cautionary tale, something to do with pride going before a fall? But there is another, more encouraging explanation: that, in spite of any possible penalties, it reflects that deepest of human needs, the great compulsion which distinguishes us from the animal world – our unremitting, passionate desire to go always a little further.

6

The Stone Dance: Corrimony

The road to Corrimony dwindled from main to secondary
and finally to a narrow farm lane running between banked
trees. It was evening when friends brought me there, a
soft grey day with shadows creeping over the pastured
fields. No house or steading could be seen, though sheep
were grazing near the low, neolithic chambered cairn. No
sound of tractors, all of them having retired to their sheds.
No visitors save ourselves. The place was silent, darkening
slowly, with only the last traces of a sun now having set.
The cairn lay close to the road, on the other side of a belt of
trees with a little wooden bridge leading over a dry ditch.
We crossed the bridge almost on tiptoe, feeling the need to
preserve that silence. We were the interlopers. 'They' – or
as it turned out, 'he' – had been resting here for nearly four
thousand years. So who were we to shout our excited
greetings?

Corrimony is one of a group of eleven similarly constructed passage-graves, all to be found near Inverness or
in the Spey valley. It is simple in design: a round central
chamber about ten feet wide, having at one time been
corbel-roofed but now with one portion open to the sky. It
was reached from the outside by a narrow passage-way
about seven feet long, a dark hole into which to wriggle.
The entire structure would originally have been covered
over with large stones and possibly turfed. Close against
the outside, forming a protective barrier and still in position,
was a low kerbstone wall, the slabs standing on edge.

We crawled warily along the tunnel, scrambling on hands and knees, the place thick with darkness, so that we emerged gladly into the small inner chamber. There was nothing for it but for us to crouch upon the sandy floor, unable as we were to avoid this act of desecration and knowing as we did that, during the 1952 excavations, stains of a crouched burial had been discovered in the sand. Again, we felt a compulsion to whisper, as if we might otherwise disturb that last inhabitant of this lonely place.

The cairn would have been constructed somewhere between 2500 and 2200 BC, but had clearly been venerated as sacred well past that period. This we realized when, not without a feeling that we might be outstaying our welcome, we struggled back into what was left of the daylight. For, having set apart a suitable space around the cairn, people of the following Bronze Age had surrounded it with one of their customary stone circles. Not a very large one, but then Corrimony, having its own magic, was not in competition with the larger, more famous complex at Balnuaran of Clava, near Inverness. These stones were low in comparison, but in common with all the Clava-type circles, the tallest had been placed at the south-west, facing the entrance to the cairn, so that the circle then sloped off towards its lowest point at the north-east. The Bronze Age people of roughly 2000 to 500 BC, although following a changing pattern of religious worship and culture, had included, here and elsewhere, the more ancient neolithic structures, certainly incorporating them into their own rituals over a period of several hundred years. There seemed to be about eleven of the circle stones still in place, though there is uncertainty about the original position of some of them. It was difficult to count them in the fading light, and I was reminded of the many legends concerning stones which get up and go off for a walk, stones which amble away to drink at night from nearby pools, stones which simply do not allow themselves to be numbered.

We spent a long time slowly walking around this lovely, isolated outpost of the Stone and Bronze Ages. We also took photographs which did not come out. Was it because of gathering dusk, or did somebody or some thing resent our modern contraptions? It was indeed a solitary place, but infinitely peaceful, set in its soft green field. It did not seem ever to have been a general burial-ground, but rather a grave or shrine for a single, and thus important, individual. This privileged inhabitant, had an element of him still clung to his sheltered tomb, would have witnessed extraordinary changes over the following four thousand years. Today the cairn is grey and solid, has a rather matter-of-fact appearance and gives an impression of independence and a determination to stay exactly where it is. It had been built to last, by people who intended that it should. Certainly the builders were conversant with the principles of architecture and must have felt a very human pride when they beheld the finished structure, gleaming whitely with its covering of unpolished quartzite stones.

We left as silently as we had come, grateful for the quietness and trusting we had let loose no disturbing influences.

Scotland, far more than England, is littered with ancient stone remains, some neatly open to view, restored and classified and carefully fenced, others protruding unnoticed from rough hillsides, half buried by centuries of peat or soil and peering at the discoverer with wild, weedy hair and clothing of lichen. In coming to the north, I had had to learn about the lives of coastal animals and birds. But the stones were immediately known and familiar, though to be encountered with a cautious respect. Glimpsing them from afar as they loomed across a deserted moorland, I felt I was returning home. Not that I had ever before crawled through the passage-way of a neolithic tomb, or walked within a Bronze Age stone circle. Nor had I ever been faced with the solitariness of a gaunt and massive megalith. Nor had I even heard of the later Pictish slabs which, with their strange carvings, bridged the three ages of a long-vanished people. No, the thing that gave familiarity to the stones, whatever their age or purpose, was just that primary quality which I can only call 'stone-ness' – the ancient, elemental substance of our planet, into the mysteries of which, because of an odd childhood addiction, I had often ventured. I held, as it were, a ticket of admission, not to be overestimated but ensuring that I should never entirely be shut out. I am often quite ignorant about actual types of stone, hesitating when faced with a varied collection of rocks, recognizing quartz or sandstone but uncertain of gneiss or schist or conglomerate. But I cherished stone, as such, from the time I was five years old, chipping one day at the wall of our house and dislodging a pretty pebble – a little white thing with strange blue geometric markings. The stone looked interesting, almost alive, and I kept it. I found others, alerted to a search which, over many summers, yielded a large collection, none of geological importance but all having certain characteristics that appealed to me: some because of their colour, some for their translucency, some for the way they shone, some for their queer contours, but many because, etched upon their surface in little cracks and lines and gradations of shading, they had faces and figures, people and animals and strange birds, a whole story in stone, a living incarnation of the fairy-tales that had nourished my imagination. Those four stalwart pillars of my childhood, Andrew Lang, Hans Andersen and the Brothers Grimm (in that order) came alive, through my mind, in the pictures and personalities with which I invested the stones I so laboriously collected, shuffling on my haunches along the rough tracks and lanes and turning over, one by one, with impenetrable attention, the possible treasures they might yield.

I was not alone. In my cousin Barbara, although she was five years older than I, I found the perfect companion for this secret world. We must have appeared extraordinary, the younger child dark and skinny, the older round and

chestnut-haired, squatting our way through the dust and
debris of the wayside, oblivious of any who might pass
inquisitively by, impervious to our mothers' embarrass-
ment. Memorable indeed was the occasion when my
cousin, returning to London by tram, spilt her box of
stones over the boarding platform so that they rolled into
the gutter, from where she insisted on recovering every
single one. The tram waited patiently.

The importance of each collection was the use to which
we put them. And here I can see that, totally disinterested
as both of us were in dolls and ordinary toys, they served us
as an acting-out, a catharsis, of our own emotions. We
played the fairy-tales, the princes and princesses of high
romance; we mimicked schools and lessons, with the 'good'
child, the 'bad' child, the 'dunce', the 'clever one'. The
variations were endless. We knew each stone intimately,
named them and loved them. We understood each special
nature and proclivity, each singular personality. Sitting at
the wooden garden table, Barbara one side and I the other,
with old chocolate and biscuit tins upturned to serve for
their 'schools' or their 'palaces', we carried out our
dramatizations in suitably modulated voices, sometimes
pursuing separate stories, sometimes interweaving with
each other, never at any moment conscious of decisions
mutually achieved, moving our charged, responsive stones
around the table, and causing them to live out their lives of
myth and fantasy from some deep spring of knowledge
sealed within us.

There were other, larger stones, almost boulders (you
might say, 'mini-megaliths'), which I lifted and carried
about with some difficulty, and which – my parents
eventually moving house and firmly rejecting them – I
buried at the bottom of the garden, sobbing inconsolably.

The stones occupied the major part of my childhood
from five until twelve or thirteen. Even then, they
remained potent symbols. And some still do, carefully
preserved in the tins which housed them in the days of

their glory. So I suppose I can say, hoping it is not too chilling an affirmation, that stones are in my blood.

There is a vast difference between stone that is lying dormant and unused upon the shore or beneath the earth, and stone that has been cut out of its resting-place, to be measured and handled and carved and carried and purposefully erected to serve the needs of a group of living people. Whatever the artefact, whether prehistoric burial cairn or medieval cathedral, something has been added, reflecting not only the enthusiasm of those who, understanding the nature of stone, had been involved in its erection, but, over centuries, a particular history imprinted upon its stones, soaked up by them and adding a subtle aura which may be of goodness or, again, may be of evil. There are people, for instance, who, on visiting Canterbury Cathedral, are acutely aware of a great darkness emanating from certain areas, though, down in the Crypt, despite encroaching commercialism, nothing can dispel the enduring holiness, an almost tangible presence, which pervades the Chapel of Our Lady Undercroft. Stones have a habit of retaining that which is put into them.

But the unshaped, untouched blocks of stone lying on our shores or leaning out of our mountains, moulded only by the natural forces of water and wind and ice, have also a history, though one in which man has played no part and left no imprint. If I stand before a large slab of old red sandstone, thrusting out of the shore and washed by the waters of the Moray Firth, I certainly cannot feel any emanations from days gone by, since – apart from the occasionally slipping gumboot – the rock has never experienced human beings. Even so, locked within its stone-ness, it contains an outer as well as an inner life, the first of which, so ancient as to be almost beyond our comprehension, is yet a part of the known world and can be discovered by all of us.

This life, since old red sandstone is a sedentary rock,
begins about 400 to 350 million years before our own time,
when sediments from the Scottish mountains were de-
posited in shallow seas, so that, gradually, over the ages,
through a process of uplifting, folding and faulting, the
sandstone lowlands of the Moray Firth, Caithness and
Orkney were built up. Rather later, but still 70 to 50 million
years ago, the compressed rock would have known a fierce
outburst of volcanic activity, with further faulting and
uplift, while as near as 3 million years the Ice Age would
have clamped down and destroyed any further development.
But as the ice sheets ebbed away some eight thousand
years ago, to form part of what is sometimes called the
Neolithic or Flandrian Sea, that sea-level rose faster than
the released land, depositing the sediments which were to
become the raised beaches of today, until, some two
thousand years later, the waters began their long process
of falling back in relation to the land.

All this my sandstone rock will have experienced, out of a
time and within a shifting consolidation of shore-line
which to us is almost unimaginable. A sedimentary rock
will have captured many early organisms, held fast now
within its structure; it will have been formed not only by
the seas and the pressure of ice, but by the immense
changes of wind and sun and temperature. It has learnt
how to endure. And here at last it sits below my cliff,
lapped and slapped by seas which, frequently rough, if not
violent, are incomparably gentler than those huge ebbings
and flowings it once had known.

There is, however, a second history contained deep
within my sandstone rock, even more ancient and mysterious. The stone is massive and quiet and unmoving, heavy
with an ageless calm. But if I could go down into the
essence of its structure, I should encounter the astonishing
world of particles. I should be lost in the untenanted spaces
existing where apparently solid substance appears before
our human eyes. Below its appearances I would enter the

unfathomable, expanding centre of matter, where atoms dissolve into pure energy. All around me would be the dust of innumerable particles, meeting and joining, releasing each other and joining again, each hurrying into an ecstatic dance of union and separation, played out in the infinitely empty spaces which surround each particle and form the solid body which is all that we are able to perceive. The clouds of delicately adjusted matter would shiver and pulse and move about each other in a timeless reciprocity. If the rock could speak, it would say: We have no stillness, only the appearance of stillness; no density, only the appearance of density; no tangible surface to be grasped, only a whirling mass of particles, each separate and distinct; no particles even, only the attraction and repulsion of elementary processes, the energy of motion. That solidity you think you touch is but illusion. Body and bones, form and structure, rocks and stars, we are shapes of light and movement. Creep down within us; compress yourself into the ultimate fragmentation of the particle, and you will find that even that particle melts into the dance of binding forces. Matter is movement. Matter is the eternal Dance.

So it would be a dangerous journey for any of us to undertake, for we should find that there are indeed no barriers. The great vibrating forms of rock, their flashing energies like distant stars, would still obey the laws of matter, cohering, each one, into the required pattern. But, glimpsed through the empty spaces of their authentic form would be the stretched expanses of the planets, the leaping flames of nebulae, the warm, dark breathing of ultimate space. No one could bear such a vision – to see the universe shimmering and blazing as pure energy become visible, transforming matter into its true components. We need the lesser miracles, the movement of particles stilled, the dissolving shapes assuming once again their immobility, the universe settling solidly about us. We need our rocks to lie quietly upon the shores of our own world, the world of concrete matter, of things and objects, defined, distinct, detached – yet always, in our imagination, to be seen and understood as insubstantial movement and beneficent grace.

7

Sea Canaries

My first glimpse of a dolphin, unexpected and not even contemplated as being a possibility, came on the third day of my moving in to the house on the cliff. Emigrating from one country to another is no small undertaking, even though in my case I was nobly assisted by a friend who had joined me on Euston Station for the long journey north. My furniture had come up well ahead of me, enthusiastically conveyed in a borrowed van by two stalwart neighbours from the south. It was February, and snow had been in the air. Had it fallen a week earlier, one could not have driven a van up the track to the house. As it was, my helpers had hastily dumped everything, taking one appalled look at the bare, howling landscape, and had duly reported that, in their opinion, the whole region was *desolate*!

But by the time I and my friend arrived, the scene had changed, as it so quickly does. The snow remained merely a threat, something you could smell but not yet see. And stretched over the dark chocolate field beside the track was a haze of pale, green-shining barley spikes, almost transparent in the weak winter sun, as if a light had been lit within each blade. The lowering clouds had politely drawn back, even if watchfully ringing the horizon in all directions. So that, sitting outside, backs against the wall as we drank our coffee in that encouraging sunshine, I had felt in a daze of satisfied accomplishment. Never mind the dark winter, which clearly hadn't left for good, spring was like me moving in. I stared smugly at what was a glittering sea, scarcely taking it in until my arm was grabbed and a voice cried wildly: 'Look! *Look*! DOLPHINS!'

I looked. And there they were, about six or seven of them, black dorsal fins piercing the crisp-waved water as they turned over and over on their way to Tarbat Ness. I gasped, jolted out of my exhausted coma. Not only were they the first I had seen from this new home, but they were the first I had ever seen. I was infatuated with all the stories about those sagacious, endearing creatures and their persistent, if at times miscalculated curiosity about the doings of mankind. We rushed to the edge of the cliff, excitedly pointing but also feeling almost reverent as they leapt black-shining from the water. I looked about me, soaking up the whole scene. Behind me lay the rich winter fields that had so distressed my earlier helpers; before me the sea was apparently dancing, as the sun was dancing, together with the rocks. All this and dolphins too!

Since then, though they are not daily passers-by, I have seen dolphins most of the time, often just a small family, sometimes in large schools of literally dozens, leaping and splashing as they take what I imagine is their morning or afternoon stroll to and from the Ness. In October, when most of them migrate for the winter, I have been lucky enough to watch them moving out, a long caravan of dark bodies strung across the water and heading down the Firth as they make for the wide opening into the North Sea. They would then be travelling around Lossiemouth, past Buckie, turning the corner at Fraserburgh and Peterhead, then out again into the deep sea, perhaps to the Baltic, as some authorities say, but perhaps further south to meet again the sun. As they pass on their exodus, cutting diagonally away from the land, they proceed rapidly and in methodical order, both young and old – no leaping, no splashing, no playful antics. Their movements are steady and rhythmic. They appear serious and concerned with their journey: out, far out, and away to their wintering in more congenial waters.

But there are always a few small families left behind to over-winter with us, and for a number of years I have kept a record, made up not only of my own reports but from the sightings of several friends living on Tarbat Ness. These I send annually to the Institute of Oceanographic Science in Surrey, which has groups of voluntary observers around the coasts of Britain. Up here we have been asked to note particularly the habits of any dolphins that remain. So the winter watch, whether from the comfort of a closed window or while struggling along the cliffs in the teeth of a gale, is therefore rather more earnest than the pleasant summer sightings.

At the back, the house faces directly over the Moray Firth, with only a short stretch of perhaps a hundred feet before the edge of the cliff. So I have an incredible view from the many rear windows, which is not surprising, since this was built as a look-out post. And although my binoculars never seem to be in the right place at the right moment, taking a look is an ongoing part of the day's activities, just in case dolphins happen to be passing or pausing for a while to graze. This is tricky for, as the coastguard himself told me, one of the first things you learn in watching the sea is that you may turn your head away at the precise moment when a distress flare goes up: in my case, when a black triangular dorsal fin is surfacing.

Our Moray Firth dolphins come from a few miles further along the coast. There, two headlands called the Sutors thrust out into a narrow strip of water connecting the Moray and Cromarty Firths, and under these cliffs dolphins have made their home. The men of the Invergordon lifeboat, leaving the Cromarty Firth for their weekly practice runs, tell us that they have never once been out through the Sutors, summer or winter, without families of dolphins immediately emerging from either side and escorting their boat into the Moray Firth. It has become a ritual. But in spite of the continual presence of dolphins in these waters, little is really known of their habits.

Certainly their mating and their births are hidden, though we know the pups are born in the summer months, around June or July. Young dolphins have often been sighted along the coast, and I heard one engaging story concerning about fifty adults, together with their offspring, grazing off Tarbat Ness, the young being kept strictly between two lines of parents so that both protection and control could be exercised over any who showed wayward tendencies.

Nowadays most people are familiar with dolphins, even if these graceful, intelligent creatures are usually confined to television and its wildlife programmes. Dozens of scientific books have been written about them, poems penned, while in novels they have featured nobly as rescuers of drowning heroines, lifting them to safety at the last moment and conveying them to the shore on their backs.

And there are the real-life stories, many of them strange and improbable, and some disconcerting until you realize that dolphins have far larger brains than humans and are accustomed to using them. They can assess and understand our needs and are prepared, not only to respond, but insist on doing do. Animal awareness of humans can be curiously unsettling: sometimes it seems as if it is we who are the unfortunates behind bars and they who are the interested spectators.

Several years ago I heard the story of a young local fisherman, out in his boat one early morning to inspect his lobster creels. He was keeping his usual careful distance from the rocky coast when suddenly – as is their habit – a thick haar came down and obliterated land and sea. He stopped his engine at once. Fog disorientates, and he was worried in case he drove on to the rocks. But there was a good swell on the sea, so that the boat was drifting anyway. This was not so good, and he began to worry. He knew only too well that there was nothing he could do, so he settled down to wait, hoping for a break in the haar. Everything seemed very still, when suddenly the boat began to lurch and shudder, and he felt rather than saw that he was surrounded by great shapes banging and butting at the sides of his small craft. He could not make out what they were, but was aware, with mounting dismay, that they were extremely powerful, ramming into him and apparently intent on wrecking the boat. Certainly they were spinning it away at considerable speed through the now churned-up waters. But again there was nothing he could do except to crouch in the middle of the boat, grasping at the side to save himself from being pitched out, while what seemed to be a desperate struggle went on around him and the shapes banged and heaved, though in an uncanny silence, and bore the shaking boat ruthlessly through the fog.

Perhaps the incident lasted only a few minutes, though it seemed more like hours, and at every moment he expected his boat to capsize as he rolled from side to side and his hands kept losing their grip. But then, in the curious way of a haar, the darkness cleared and he came out into open water with the sun glancing down and the fog dispersed – and saw, to his amazement, a number of dolphins turning over and over and leaping into the air as they made off, rapidly, about their own daily business. It was then, as he looked about him, that he realized how near to the rocks his boat had been drifting, and understood that the dolphins had deliberately come to his rescue.

What is so extraordinary about the story is the way in which the dolphins can be seen to have used their minds to appreciate the young fisherman's situation. Not only had they pushed him, however roughly, far out into deep water, but they must have been well aware of his danger: perceiving what was, of course, no danger for them. They had also understood that he himself was not able actually to see that danger, and that in any case he was helpless to do anything about it. So they had gathered round in a common effort to succour this vulnerable creature from what, as they alone could tell, might otherwise have been his destruction upon those rocks.

Sometimes I think that if the human race manages to succeed in wrecking its own environment, it will be the dolphins that will take over; perhaps even returning to the land from which they once came and developing their skills along rather more peaceful lines than we have so far managed to do. When one comes to think about it, and considers the greenhouse effect and the possible swamping of continents by the melting of the poles, maybe the dolphins will not need very much adjustment. They can become once more land-sea creatures, using their enlarged watery territory, uncontaminated then by oil spillage or nuclear waste, while quietly, slowly, gently, gracefully, over hundreds of thousands of years, enhancing their immense powers of reasoning so that they become, eventually, earth's inheritors, having perhaps accepted some of our rather better human tendencies while being careful to avoid those that have led us so frequently to disaster. The whole process could well lead to a renewal of that earlier Garden where there was no separation of creaturely beings, no loss of communication. Indeed, if the Lord God chose once again to walk there in the cool of the day, he might well sigh with relief. 'Adam!' he would say, and 'Eve!' – surveying those resplendent beings – 'This time, take also of the tree of life, and eat, and live for ever.'

Meanwhile the dolphins have to put up with our ignorant ways, submitting with indulgent patience when taken from their own vast environment and dumped into small pools where, in order to amuse the paying public, they are encouraged to jump through hoops and play with coloured balls. Paradoxically, it is this very exploitation which has led to so much interest and affection for them. Perhaps one day it may also lead to a rather more dignified relationship with these co-residents of our planet.

As I walk along the cliff or look from a window from a decent distance and with binoculars, what am I seeing? All those books with all those delightful pictures, telling in graphic detail about the various named species, their length, their shape, their colour, their happy hunting-grounds. How confusing they are! For the actual creature in the sea does not obligingly stand still for you to check its special markings; nor does it wait for you to bring out a tape-measure to record its length. So how do I know what I am looking at, when I see a black dorsal fin appearing for a second or two? How do I know what its name is, as the great shining creature leaps clear into the sky, then curves over and dives deep beneath the water? The answer is that I don't. But even so, there are clues to be followed. To begin with, you learn to discard porpoises, which are only about six feet long and very stubby and small when seen at a distance out to sea. Also, they rarely leap. So we can seize instead upon the common dolphin. However, they are only about eight feet long, and though prolific in the English Channel, are not seen so often in the far north.

But if it is not the common dolphin, who is the owner of that sketchily seen dorsal fin? When I began to dolphin watch, I was advised to get the measurement of a regularly seen fishing-boat and to carry that in my mind's eye when trying to estimate the length of a passing dolphin. The usual morning fishing-boat turned out to be fourteen feet long, which proved a useful guide, and I began, waveringly, to come down on the white-sided dolphin, which measures up rather better with its ten feet or so of length. I checked on other details, and now remain fairly confident that I may have pinned it down. Certainly the pale under-markings can easily be seen in their constant leaping. They are known to live in schools of about fifty, though larger numbers are often sighted. All this would fit nicely, since there have been huge companies off Tarbat Ness, and as one friend put it, 'The sea was boiling with them!' Also, the local fishermen are emphatic that what we are seeing around this coast are dolphins of up to twelve feet in length, and they are far more competent than I at estimating size, and come much closer to dolphins in their boats than I do upon my cliff. So I come down, after years of changing my mind, on the side of the white-sided dolphin.

It was a few years ago, when I was scrambling one very early morning along the lower part of the cliff, that I saw a strange procession moving rapidly up the Moray Firth, close inshore. I had left the house and gone out into a sparkling summer day, the rocks and grass and bushes washed with light. I was following a more or less horizontal sheep-trod, stumbling over knotty roots of whin while being continually caught by the prickles and struggling not to trip and slither over the edge of the path. In fact I was having a splendid time, feeling very six-o'clockish and keeping my eyes, perhaps unwisely, on the glittering sea rather than on the path. Even so, the swiftly moving progress of nine or ten dolphins, so close below, took me by surprise. They had come up behind me, thrusting through the water, intensely black against the morning light as they surged along at speed just beyond the rocks. They were not leaping but rearing up with tremendous strength, and for the first time I realized what it means when a dolphin is travelling fast: they can easily manage twenty to twenty-five knots.

I paused to get my breath, uncertain of what I was seeing, knowing that these were different from the usual families along this coast; knowing them to be strangers in a strange sea, and instinctively sensing that they carried themselves with a princely air. Yet I was puzzled as to what they were and whence they could have come. Then I discovered just how different they were, for, as they repeatedly surfaced, keeping together in a tight formation, I could see not only that they were huge but that their heads ended in a peculiarly long beak, jutting out like a truncheon as they breasted the waves.

I watched as long as I could, stumbling after them along

the rough sheep-trod and trying to keep pace, until they outdistanced me. I was filled now with a rising excitement because finally I had realized that what I had seen were exalted members of *Tursiops truncatus*, the bottle-nosed dolphin, so rarely reported now from the increasingly polluted Moray Firth. At one time there were large numbers in both the Dornoch and Moray Firths, but North Sea drift fishing-nets, as well as hazardous chemicals and oil spillage, have decimated them (as other dolphins, too). The small school now passing would probably have journeyed across the top of Sutherland and Caithness in order to come down into the Firth as summer visitors, though they might just possibly have been one of the few remaining resident families. These infinitely graceful and slender creatures, sometimes more than twelve feet in length and living for almost twenty-five to thirty years, are highly intelligent, with an acute sense of mimicry and a keen interest in man: we have to hope that man will take an equally keen interest in their diminishing chances of preservation.

I peered after them longingly, but soon they were gone, leaving me far behind with a memory of great, swift beings going about their own mysterious affairs. Then I sat down upon a rock, watching a sea now emptied of their presence and savouring those dramatic moments as they had swept imperiously by. I wished I could have caught their attention. I had tried a little singing, but, unlike seals, they were too intent upon their journey to stop and listen. It struck me then, what a difference there is between seals and dolphins, the seals having one great advantage, the ability to remove themselves temporarily from the sea, whether sunning upon a rocky coast or, more importantly, when giving birth to their pups. Dolphins, in common with all whales, are unable to do this, leading to the many recorded strandings when they have been beached and unable to retreat into the water. The common porpoise, the bottle-nosed dolphin and the common dolphin, in that

order, are each reported as having been the most frequently
stranded. Another unlucky group, the false killer dolphin –
great creatures of sixteen feet long which properly belong
to the oceans – sometimes venture into coastal waters
where they meet their fate. A large school of 150 was
discovered in 1927, having run themselves ashore in our
Dornoch Firth.

All dolphins are, of course, whales – though, equally, not
all whales are dolphins. The huge creatures of the distant
oceans are vast in size by comparison with a six-foot
porpoise, yet they all share a second distinction from seals:
being entirely water-borne, they have no need to support
their own weight and therefore can, and in some species
do, attain far greater size than any land or partly land
animal could ever achieve.

During the summer of 1988 a single beluga, or white
whale, hit the national headlines because it had ventured
into the Moray Firth and then decided, out of sheer
curiosity, to pause awhile and inspect the three seaboard
villages a few miles along the coast from where I live.
Technically, a beluga is a dolphin (*Delphinapterus leucas*), a
mammal of up to eighteen feet, coloured all over in delicate
creamy white. Like its near-counterpart, the narwhal, it
belongs truly to the Arctic, being almost entirely circum-
polar and visiting our waters only accidentally. Therefore its
appearance in the Moray Firth, if only for a day or two, was
an exciting event. Perhaps wisely, it did not tempt
providence by outstaying its welcome, and I regretted
deeply that I had not caught a glimpse of this lovely dolphin
as it journeyed back northwards into the open sea. It would
certainly have passed the house, and though Halley and I
might well have been on the cliff, it was clearly one of those
occasions on which, for a moment, I must have turned my
head.

Halley, being a huntress and therefore keenly aware of

all that goes on both in the sea and on the land, is, I fear, intensely jealous of all dolphins. There was one bright February morning when we were walking above the shore and came out on to a sharp point of cliff with a wide view over the Firth. There had been dolphins earlier, with the day clouded, but now the sun was shining and they had decided to enjoy it, dozens and dozens of them surfacing to greet the warmth. Dolphins always appear keenly sensitive to sunlight. They will surface, it is true, in stormy water with grey skies, but then it is usually a sign that the rough weather is about to subside. And when the sunlight really does flood down upon the sea, you can almost feel the ecstatic welcome they give it, leaping and splashing and chasing each other as if delighted to throw off the grey skies as well as the grey waters.

On this particular day these were very large dolphins, silvery sided as well as silver underneath, and so almost certainly the white-sided variety. In their leaping, one of them shot up so high that it came down absolutely straight into the water, looking like a great steel penknife. I stood on the edge of the cliff, watching for about half an hour, but being constantly interrupted by Halley. She could see the dolphins even better without binoculars than I could with them! She knew they were taking my whole attention and, as her jealousy mounted, she divided her time between mewing piteously while wreathing and writhing about my gumboots, and sitting malevolently on the very edge of the cliff, glaring at the oblivious creatures below.

There have been so many lovely dolphin days, when they have cruised slowly along the coast, often staying for a time in one patch of water, grazing. In time you get used to them as welcome passers-by, though the excited cry of 'Dolphins!' (or, from visitors, 'What are those black things jumping out of the water?') never fails to send you rushing for the binoculars. They do not, as do seals (and this is another distinction), have voices, but sometimes we have heard the high-pitched whistling sounds that occur when

they are completely under water. Apparently this is caused
when a fine stream of bubbles escapes through their blow-
hole. Indeed, the beluga, when below the surface, makes a
low, trilling sound, 'reminiscent of the cry of curlews in the
spring time',* which led the old-time whalers to call them
'sea canaries'.

Although lacking 'voices' as such, dolphins are equipped
with high-frequency sound-producing apparatus through
which they communicate with each other and even mimic,
to a certain extent and while in captivity, the human voices
of their captors. Recent experiments have led scientific
observers to suggest that the very large brain of, for
instance, the bottle-nosed dolphins – about thirty per cent
larger than the human brain – may have potential speech
capabilities which could conceivably resemble our own.
This opens up all kinds of alarming possibilities and *Tursiops
truncatus* would surely be well advised to resist all inducements towards fluent intercourse with humans. The
prospect of the eventual introduction of radio programmes
beamed into the oceans of the world for the edification of
the dolphin young does not bear thinking about!

Of all my dolphin watchings, during the years I have spent
on this cliff, the most memorable experience I have had –
even more moving than my glimpse of those Atlantic
adventurers – was on one summer evening when a group
of young men arrived, laden with diving equipment. Their
aim was to locate the sunken battleship lodged, it was
believed, in that last chasm of the Great Glen Fault. Having
donned their apparatus, which had meant carrying heavy
oxygen packs along and down the cliff, they set off under
water. It was a windless evening, with a sheet of flat blue silk

---

* Quoted by L. Harrison Matthews, op. cit., from W. E. Schevill and B.
Lawrence, 'Underwater listening to the white porpoise (*Delphinapterus
leucas*)', Science, 109 (1949), 143–4.

for sea. I could just trace the swimmers' tracks, while every now and then the leader would surface and I would see the scarlet of his breathing gear. There wasn't much to watch, nothing spectacular, and certainly no likelihood of any battleship so close to the shore. I sat placidly on the edge of the cliff with the sun slanting low behind me.

And then, coming in diagonally from the east, far out across the entrance to the Firth, I saw a long, straight line of dolphins, almost, it seemed, in single file. There must have been about fifty of them, and they would have come from over near Lossiemouth and be heading home to the Sutors. On and on they pressed, dark specks which rapidly became larger as they pursued an unswervingly straight course.

The leading swimmer, below the surface, must have been at least half a mile short of the leading dolphin when suddenly, without a flicker of hesitation, the whole column, as if actuated by a single command, swung slowly, deliberately, into a deepening curve towards the swimmers. They had sensed something new. They had decided to investigate. So on they came, the whole formation sweeping in a great bow across the sea. I watched as if it were taking place upon a stage, and presently the leading swimmer shot up to the surface, tiny and infinitely fragile, confronting the leading dolphin. Immediately he was encircled by the rest. It was a moment of pure drama, the young man obviously quite unafraid, the dolphins serious and inquisitive, the whole encounter being played out between sea intruder and sea dwellers as they looked and listened and took stock of each other. Then, after about two or three minutes, and having evidently decided that the interloper posed neither threat nor was of any particular interest, the leading dolphin swung away, back on to that direct course across the Firth. The rest fell in smoothly behind him, the great curve became once more a straight line, and the long procession continued on its way.

Later, when the would-be divers had returned from their otherwise fruitless expedition, the young man sat on the cliff, excited and breathless, face shining as he recounted the experience with enraptured delight. To be there, far out, in the midst of that quiet water. To be surrounded by those dark, perceptive inhabitants of the sea. To be inspected courteously and with due attention; acknowledged as one whose purposes were just as beneficent as their own. This, we agreed, is how it should always be. Two groups of very different creatures meeting, saluting each other, and then continuing their private and separate journeys.

8

Felis or Felix?

Those summer evenings are long and still and golden, with the late-setting sun moving far into the north. But in winter it is a different tale, when the dark begins to shut down soon after 3.30. This means that any expeditions out of doors, unless there is a moon, are ventures into a blacked-out world, so that one must carry a torch which, only too often, produces either an irritating hiccup – on, off – or the faintest of dying gleams which scarcely illumine your feet. So you get used to sensing your way. Anyhow, during twelve years you should have become familiar with the terrain. And it must be said that your stumbling progress towards the coal-bunker or the freezer shed brings its own rewards. One of the strangest, most magical of these is to be had walking around the corner of the house and hearing, quite suddenly, the harsh honking and creaking wing-beats of wild swans flying down from the north. You do not see them in the pitchy dark, but you can tell they are coming in low across the garden, then lifting a little and changing course. At first the cries are distant, but steadily the sound increases. There is the whirring, rhythmic push of heavy bodies moving just above your head and only the other side of the fence. The darkness has the momentary imprint of a different layer of dark. Then, like the Doppler shift of a train whistle, the sound changes and slowly dies. You are left standing there alone, conscious that invisible strangers have passed by from a distant and more icy winter world than your own, leaving no traces except, you might say, that they came with snow on their boots.

There are other, smaller noises: the soft scufflings of such mice and shrews as have escaped Halley's attentions; the squawk of a disturbed sea-gull; the crunch of a sheep's teeth; the hasty, plunging scamper of some unidentifiable scavenger of the night. Out in the Firth there may be an oil-rig platform, towed away to the North Sea after its servicing in Invergordon: an enchanting sight, since its huge, pointed superstructure is lit up from top to bottom with a thousand lights, so that it appears like a brilliantly decorated Christmas tree floating silently and majestically past. You look about you, noting other, single lights from farm or cottage, each conveying its own particular message of people at home. And through it all, the regular four flashes of the lighthouse and the long, dark wait for the next batch.

Sometimes in my nocturnal ramblings I can watch the unfolding play of the 'Merry Dancers', seen when the winter sky is clear and hard and frosted; great veils and curtains of shifting light spreading across the sky from north-east to north-west, and falling from about six hundred miles above the earth's surface to almost sixty, seeming to brush the hills. 'Merry' seems hardly a suitable word for such a vast and complicated phenomenon. What apparently happens, according to modern views, is that solar particles, discharged at times of sun-spot flares, enter and interact with the great magnetic 'belts' which surround the earth. These belts, becoming overloaded, then 'dump' some of their particles into the atmosphere: to be seen as those amazing curtains, arcs, streamers and draperies of light and colour which we call the auroras. In France the dancers are known, more freakishly, as *chèvres dansantes*, the dancing goats, which accords better with the strangeness of the spectacle, beautiful yet somehow dangerous, as if having to do with witchcraft. There is the legend of James, Earl of Derwentwater, who in 1716 was beheaded for rebellion – an event which is said to have conjured up, that night, an unusually brilliant display of the dancing goats.

It is in winter that the night sky is at its most enticing, being sharp and dark yet illumined by the faint dust of stars. I can set up my small telescope on the cliff-top at a reasonable evening hour, which would be impossible during summertime with the sun going down so late. In winter, too, the constellations are more brilliant, though the viewing is infinitely more painful than it would be in kinder months. Even when the wind is not actually blowing the tripod over, it means much rubbing of numbed fingers, gasping through woolly mufflers and stamping of well-socked if increasingly chilly boots. But the rewards are great. The crackling bitterness of a deep winter's dark offers the whole glory of the night sky.

It is true that, in rather more comfort, I can even watch from my bed as Orion hunts above the Moray Firth, or the moon curves high across the window-pane, washing the whole room with light. But it needs the telescope to open up the sky in ways never before so clearly known. Then the moon will no longer be that shining plate, but is revealed as an enormous and slightly shocking globe of whitened stone, hanging there heavily, as if at any moment it might lose its balance and plunge down the sky. You ask yourself, how does it stay up? And it needs the telescope to discover, some 480 million miles away, the magic silver ball of Jupiter, flanked by four of the twelve satellites, each infinitesimally changing position as it drifts behind or before the glittering presence. There is Saturn, lying sideways like a schoolgirl's wide-brimmed straw hat. The Pleiades, appearing not as the usual fuzz but as a stretch of jewelled netting, spangled with huge stars. There is Polaris, the pole-star of the north, solitary and, in the not too distant future of twelve thousand years, to be displaced, its primacy overtaken when the earth's wobble focuses instead on Vega, the brilliant blue star in the constellation of Lyra.

Not that the night sky is new to me in the way that seals and dolphins and other creatures have been since my coming to Scotland. My fascination with it had early beginnings. When I was nine years old I was taken by my mother to visit a friend's home, where I was offered, presumably to keep me quiet, a school atlas. It was just the ordinary collection of world maps, but before they began I found something I had never seen: a half-page devoted to 'astronomical geography'. And there they all were, sun and stars and planets. There, too, was our own world, swinging in a huge ellipse around the sun, bordered by such esoteric terms as 'vernal equinox' and 'summer solstice'. There, before my dazzled eyes, was the great solar system depicted on a few inches of shiny paper, the planets eddying away from each other into the cold reaches of outer space; the eclipses of sun and moon; the cramped maps of the northern and southern heavens; the black-and-white juggler's balls of the phases of the moon.

Across all these years I can still feel, as if it were only this morning, the sensation of a mortal body blow, the breath caught back in my throat, my mind split wide open with the awareness of infinity. It was for me a revelation very like the moment which must have bludgeoned St Paul on the Damascus road. Something had entered into my bones, had washed through my bloodstream, had taken over and occupied me; something which most certainly had nothing to do with education (for which I did not care very much) but which, though I did not know it, had everything to do with religion.

Whatever I had been able to accept of organized worship during my life has left me far from orthodox, even though, in my twenties, I committed myself to a rare, once-in-a-blue-moon church community that offered all of us who belonged to it then (and who still belong to each other and that church's vision now) a foretaste of what our world should properly be. I have added but I have also discarded. So my present religious beliefs are perhaps a curious mishmash, though I find a satisfying basis in that early recognition of infinity. Indeed, religion makes no sense to me unless seen under this enormous movement of the universe. The night sky up in this clear atmosphere is vast, the horizon unencumbered by buildings and unstained by city lights. I turn full circle and am caught up into a huge inverted bowl of stars. Each constellation of our northern hemisphere is seen in a reality now transferred from the pictured page, and can be followed as it travels around the sky, rising and setting and deceptively presenting itself as encircling our world. The galaxies, glimpsed through the interstices of our Milky Way, move with them, seemingly fixed. Yet they are rushing headlong across space, further and further into nothingness, fleeing into the dark night of the universe, so that the ancient music of the spheres, the dance of particles, confronts us with a message that transcends all we think and affirm.

As I look up at what is going on above my head, I can observe, so far as my limited understanding coupled with a moderate telescope can probe, the whole mystery of time and space, the fearful, blinding dignity of infinitely distant worlds, wheeling at incredible, unfaltering speeds. I can take account of our own comparatively insignificant planetary system, moving rhythmically and always within its established pattern, lying on the lonely perimeter of an enormously tight-packed galaxy of densely circling stars ('tight' only to our limited vision). That is miracle enough to rule out, for me, the ludicrously inadequate suggestion that it came about by 'accident'. So far as I can tell, the whole thing reeks of 'purpose', and a purpose demands an intelligence. That awkward old problem! Scientifically, we argue between the theories of 'steady growth' or 'big bang' to explain the origin of the universe, as if a clear decision has only to be made and whichever is chosen will give us the ultimate answer. But of course there is no answer. Not for us. Not at any rate on this small planet. For while the facts elucidated by our scientific investigations must indeed be included within the answer, they are certainly not the whole story and do not even begin to solve the question 'Why?' Why the big bang? The mystery is surely beyond our comprehension. But at least, if we prefer 'purpose' to 'accident', we have then to speculate about the way in which the purposer, or Creator, chose to bring his universe into being. Perhaps he began by 'pressing the button' (an ominous phrase, yet certainly what happened then makes a nonsense of our own nuclear tinkerings) to initiate that big bang from which the universe developed over aeons along the permitted lines of its own natural physical laws; we, the human beings, having evolved at approximately the last minute, being a part of all that was intended.

And here, of necessity, we tip over into myth and symbol. We may use the modern jargon of pressing buttons, or the equally mystifying but rather more attractive picture of the Creator standing upon the void and ordering the neat arrangement of light and dark, day and night, heaven and earth, water and land. The one interprets the other; both are expressions, the one scientific, the other poetic, of how the universe came about. There need be no quarrel between them.

My own belief is in a Creator who does not stand outside the universe he has willed, contemplating it as might the painter of a picture or the architect of a cathedral. On the contrary, he contains within himself all that is. We and our worlds are part of the structure of his being. Just as red and white corpuscles circulate within our veins and arteries, so the galaxies circulate within the *Corpus Dei*. The stars are his vesture. The universe, as its component parts fly outward at unthinkable speeds, expands with an enormous out-breathing, fractionally avoiding such rapidity as would cancel all possibility of return, and, for the time being, avoiding also an in-breathing which would (will?) draw all creation back into one primal point. We are indeed 'feathers on the breath of God'.

All this makes sense to me, and if it sounds incongruous

with what we know of scientific evolution, or indeed with Church teaching, I suggest that there are two aspects of truth: the truth of fact and the truth of imagination. Both are equally and coexistingly valid. Both are reconcilable. The one, invisible to us, is the 'lining' of that other which we think of, here, as being reality. But the garment is reversible. At present, through our inadequate senses of touch and sight and smell and taste and hearing, we experience one side only of what may turn out to be many different realities. I see this as an exhilarating prospect.

But in winter, it is not only the night sky, not only the mystery of creation, which rivets one's attention. There are other, lesser happenings which demand instant investigation and involvement. And you have to be ready for them. One of these, for Edward and me, was the coming of the wild cat. But that took place later, and first there was the strange story of a small cat living wild in a farm-steading. It had not been born wild, and I had sometimes seen it, a neat, tortoise-shell little creature that had belonged across the field in a farm cottage – quite happily, as I had supposed. But one day she walked out on her devoted protectors, having decided to 'go feral'. No inducements served to lure her back to the comforts of a now desolated household, and from then on she lived in sin among the huge straw bales of the nearest farm. Here she recklessly produced litter after litter of wildly unapproachable young. And I well remember a certain hard winter in which I unexpectedly became involved in her random way of life. I was up at the farm one late evening and had gone outside to offer a good-night apple to the owner's pony. It was snowing, large, soft, insidious flakes idling down out of a black sky. The yard lights were on, but diffused into that smudgy blur which accompanies snow or fog, visibility being down to a few feet around each light. There I could see that the snow had thickened, falling with apparent weightlessness, unhastening yet irresistible. Beyond the patches of half-light lay a wall of darkness blotting out all contact with the rest of the farm, so that I seemed to be standing in a complete void, the buildings dissolved, and nothing existing but that pale circle of light.

But I knew my way back, and was returning to the house when I heard, through the padded silence of the steading, a sharp little cry, a sudden, imperative call for help. I stopped dead in my tracks, turning and staring back across the yard. All I could make out was that dim pool of light extending for about five yards before the dark took over. I went on staring, beginning now to feel chilled and wanting only to hurry on towards the warm house. I had already turned away when it came once more, that fierce, thin, appealing cry. So I hesitated, peering back from beneath white-furred eyelids and suddenly, on the very edge of the light, a small dark shape appeared, heading towards me with steady determination. It was the little tortoise-shell cat, picking her way firmly across the yard, her back white with snow, her tail high and stiff, as if she were holding out a flag of distress. She came straight to me, mewing softly now, and stopped a couple of yards from my feet, looking up at me as if trying to tell me something. Then she turned and deliberately walked away, back in the direction from which she had come, not pausing, not looking round, totally certain that I would follow.

I watched her for a few seconds, so tiny and somehow so full of purpose, and thought I had never seen any creature so alone and in such obvious need. But the whole point was that she was not alone, and, dragging my torch out of my pocket, I plunged after her, frightened lest I lost sight of where she was taking me. We crossed the yard, and I kept the torch dipped to the ground just short of her receding, stubborn figure. We turned down the lane between the sheds, across another yard, and into an open doorway. The place was packed high with bales of straw, and as we entered, we were met by a crescendo of high-pitched squealings as a horde of tiny kittens sprang out of the caverns and tunnels of the stacks. The mother cat looked up at me. Then, rubbing against my gumboots, her tail waving triumphantly, she told me, as plainly as if she had spoken, what her difficulties were.

'Yes, yes!' I gulped, bending down and rubbing the snow off her back. 'Yes, oh yes! Of course. Just hold on. I'll be back. I'll not be long. Truly! I'm not leaving you. I'll be back as soon as I can!'

With which I turned and ran, while she watched me from the doorway, clearly undisturbed at my hasty exit, and trusting, as with human beings she had always been in the habit of trusting, that I would attend at once to her needs. Back at the house I rapidly prepared two large deep plates of bread and milk, not too hot and not too cold, and out again I rushed, terrified of slipping on the now-impacting snow and dropping the lot, but managing to hurry back successfully to that famished little family. When I got there, the mother cat was sitting by the door, obviously waiting for me. Of the kittens, there was no sign. But as soon as I placed one of the food-platters on the ground, there was a rustling and a squeaking and six thin, furry bodies descended in a shower upon the saving food. Nobody fought, nobody even pushed. It was all too urgent for that. Each little body simply fixed itself to an inch or so of plate and began desperately to lap its shivering way through what lay in front of it. The mother cat stood aloof, watching carefully, and making no attempt to grab any of it. So then I put down her own plate, at a little distance from the kittens and – I could almost hear the sigh of thankfulness – she settled down to eat her way solidly through every little bit.

Yes, she was now a feral cat, but in her extremity something had surfaced of an earlier trust in humans, something of remembered comfort and warmth and food in plenty always dispensed by them. It had sent her out into the snow, perhaps when she heard my voice as I talked to the pony, or my muffled footsteps as I turned away from the steading. And she had sought me out with the absolute certainty that I would heed her cries and that her young would be provided for. 'Come with me. Now!' she had demanded, peremptorily, but with the remnants of feminine appeal, laying hold of me with all the strength of her small, undefeated person. She knew without a shadow of doubt that I was bound to follow.

It is not often that we have snow on this cliff-top, certainly not deep snow that lies for weeks. I am always sorry about this, since I love a snowy world almost more than any other kind. But what we are more frequently offered in winter is a dark, wild world with storm-force winds. Then, to call it dark is an understatement, for a winter night on the edge of the cliff can be pitch-black, the clouds lying on top of the house like a dustbin lid, blotting out the stars and, if it is also raining, allowing no glimpses of the gold chain of little towns across the water.

And when the wind has been blowing steadily for two or more days and nights, varying between Gale Force 10 and Storm Force 12, it is a comfort to know that the hatches are all well battened down – all the inside window-shutters braced in position and the two glass doors, front and back, padded with heavy curtains. I sit with my book before a huge fire, partly of coal but mostly of logs and compressed peat, the latter being my guilty attempt to avoid emitting sulphur fumes into the already polluted atmosphere. Though I am only too well aware that you cannot win at that game. So, the fire roars fiercely to meet the wilder roar of the wind outside. This incredible, thunderous racket, magnified in the chimney, lasts for hours on end, the noise being exactly as if I were standing on a station platform when an express train goes hurtling through. And though it is mainly produced by the westerlies, tearing in from the Atlantic and slamming along the side of the house, I have to concede that, on this eastern cliff, the winter easterlies are infinitely worse. They come racing through the Moray Firth's wide opening into the North Sea, hitting the top of the cliff and bouncing over the edge with redoubled fury. The rear windows wave to and fro like glass curtains, so that the reflected room, seen against the storm's black sky, jerks and jumps alarmingly, and if I place my hand against that pane, I can feel it thrumming.

This is the time – when you can tell exactly that it is Force 11 – to hasten around the house, fixing those thin wooden shields which, while they cannot prevent a window breaking, will certainly halt the resulting slivers of glass from slicing across the room at top speed. Quite often the wilder winds spring up out of nowhere as instantaneously as they die away, and I have frequently been awakened in the middle of the night to feel the whole building rattling and rocking, the floor shaking beneath the bed. It is reassuring to know that the walls are of heavy stone, two-foot thick, but the windows are quite another matter, especially when you have gone to bed without putting up the shutters and must, at perhaps three o'clock in the morning, stagger blindly around to remedy that big mistake. It always sounds much worse in the night.

But the night the wild cat came, it was a dark and unusually quiet evening. The room was peaceful and I could see Edward sitting outside on the stone window-sill. It was a corner window, relatively protected from wind and weather, and Edward's chosen perch. Here he could command all that was happening: he had a clear view down to the end of the garden, where the stile led over the fence to the edge of the cliff, and, turning his handsome golden head, a keen appreciation of what was going on inside, in what friends call 'the Snug'. He had the very best of both worlds, since a single mew would suffice to bring his slave running to open the nearby door, yet, should he wish to go off hunting, this course of action could be immediately embarked upon without his having to insist on being let out. There is always this difficulty with cats: in, out; in out;

let me in at the front door so that I may walk straight
through to be let out at the back.

On this particular night, however, harmony had been
achieved, and I read steadily on, conscious now and then
of a great orange hump settled solidly the other side of the
window-pane. So it was with sudden shock that I heard
Edward's dreadful howl. It was not the usual caterwauling
wrangle between two argumentative animals, moaning
away into a crescendo of hideous chords and inevitably
ending in the spitting and snarling of a cat-fight. No. This
was an animal stung violently into intense fear and
desperation.

I jumped up, seeing him now reared upon the window-
sill, about twice his usual size, enormous with fluffed-up
gold fur and his great back hooped in terrified confrontation.
I seized a torch and rushed to the back door. Opening it, I
was almost knocked flying by the resourceful Edward
(always choosing discretion rather than valour), who shot
between my legs into the safety of the house.

Outside, everything was still – except for my shaking.
The night was silent and heavy and nothing stirred. Then,
fleetingly, I caught a faint colouring of dark upon dark and,
switching on the torch, saw a large grey shadow moving
slowly, disdainfully, across the lawn towards the stile. At a
distance of about five yards the shadow turned and faced
the torchlight, and I saw my first wild cat. It was
magnificent. Large, much larger than I had thought them
to be, and grey with deep, dark-banded fur and a wide, flat
head, ears lowered menacingly, eyes yellow and cold and
indifferent. The tail drooped around its heavy back legs, a
ringed plume almost as thick as a fox's brush. We regarded
each other for a few moments in silent concentration.
Then, somehow, the shadow was no longer there, only
the grass in the torchlight, and the stile, and the bushes at
the edge of the cliff. I returned to the house to comfort
Edward, who was not amused.

I saw the wild cat on two further nights, once close up

against the front porch, vaguely in the evening dusk, then again, slipping ghostlike around the corner of the house. Since then, save for a sudden movement of something large and grey down on the shore one late afternoon, which might or might not have been our visitor, it seems that *Felis sylvestris* has not returned. If it had, Edward would have known. The burden frequently borne by a doctored male cat is that of being attacked without any other provocation by a 'whole' animal, which resents the deprived one with furious disgust. Once before Edward had been severely savaged by a farm cat, a much heavier animal which had forced him down a narrow gap behind a shed, so that the attacker was uppermost and the unfortunate Edward was on his back, wedged into a crevice and fighting, literally, for his life. On that dreadful evening, armed with a heavy stick but not daring to use it in case I jabbed Edward, I managed to confuse the attacker by directing my torch full into his eyes. Edward escaped, torn and bleeding. After it was all over and the aggressor had made off, I sat with Edward in my lap for nearly an hour before he was able to gain any control at all over his frantically laboured breathing. Then, and then only, could I attend to his wounds.

In thinking about Edward and comparing him with Halley (and also with that little feral mother cat), I can see that though Halley has been doctored (the very thought of an endless supply of kittens made my blood run cold), she has retained every last ounce of her incorrigible femininity – even preferring, should she condescend to accept a welcoming knee, a male one to a female, and then becoming outrageously flirtatious. Sometimes I wonder how kind our well-meant attentions are to those house cats we ignorantly believe we have tamed. Perhaps we need them far more than they need us. And perhaps *Felis sylvestris*, now only to be found (within Britain) in the north of Scotland, is truly more of a *Felix sylvestris* than is his comfortable, dependent counterpart. After all, as Kipling has told us, the

wild cat is the 'Cat that Walked by Himself, walking by his
wild lone through the Wet Wild Woods and waving his wild
tail'. Certainly, a good living can still be obtained up on
these wet wild cliffs. And the tail of the *Felis/Felix sylvestris*
is a splendid tail for waving.

It is an ever-present dilemma, this domesticating of a
basically wild creature. It can, and so often does, lead to a
wonderfully reciprocal relationship, with true affection on
both sides. Yet in the end, the house-pet, even in such a
situation of mutual trust, has to pay for its abandonment of
wildness. Paradoxically, it pays because it becomes in-
tuitively involved with us. Edward eventually paid, for he
knew exactly the moment of his death. And it was I who
communicated it to him, holding him in my arms as the vet
clipped his fur to bare the place into which the needle
would mercifully slide. In that moment Edward howled,
weaving his head from side to side in total rejection and
continuing with his cries and the shaking of his head until
the needle had allowed his spirit to escape. We looked at
each other then, the vet and I, and his face had gone white
as he said: 'He cried like a child. He knew what we were
doing.' Yes indeed, for I, through my grief, had told him.

Everyone who has had to endure the deliberate dying of
however sick an animal, has always to meet the burden of
guilt that inevitably ensues. It is the kind of guilt that can
only swamp us when we are face to face with a non-human
creature to whom we cannot explain matters. We alone
have to make the choice. We do not know (though, in that
last moment, I did know) what he himself would have
chosen. So, we act. Was the decision too precipitate? Should
those cries have prevailed? There is no easy answer. You
do what you believe must be done to prevent a beloved
animal lingering in constant pain. Yet the guilt remains.
And the loss.

But there is one final and all-important reflection.
Whatever the cost of this companionship to him, there is,
between cat and self, no such thing as one-sidedness.

There is relationship, involvement, each with the other; speaking together, albeit in different tongues; an intelligent exchange which brings enrichment to both. Edward enriched me in subtle ways which neither he nor I could have foreseen, and which remain, for both, an inscrutable mystery.

9

The Stone Dance: Callanish

I had been eleven years on my cliff-top before being able to make a pilgrimage to Callanish, the great stone circle on the Island of Lewis in the Hebrides, but at last it was arranged and I set forth with friends from the south, equally besotted with stones and also on a first journey to the islands. We had done our homework, with all those weighty tomes and condensed booklets, the art volumes and the paperbacks. We had noted the many aerial photographs of the unique cross-shaped grouping of megaliths: a central circle with four radiating arms, some incomplete, one of them a long avenue of massive stones pointing to the north. And we were aware that the cross had nothing to do with Christianity, the stones having been erected several thousand years before the Christian religion came into being. There were arguments for and against the circle's having been an astronomical observatory, geared to produce an accurate calendar, and we had decided that this idea seemed exceedingly doubtful. Also, I at any rate was of the opinion that Callanish would prove to be not just next in rank to Stonehenge but infinitely greater: more mysterious, more enigmatic, more abundantly alive. Like all fanatics we had our opinions and were going to stick to them. Callanish, for all of us, was out of this world.

So we set off, and when we arrived at the Kyle of Lochalsh during that summer of 1988, I was to discover that there had been changes since I had travelled this way in 1935. I remembered the earlier occasion vividly: an end-of-the-road gravelly slope into the water, where, waiting patiently, was a small wooden raft with an engine attached. On to this we had driven across a plank drawbridge, nosing our way up front in mortal terror of continuing over the end, and leaving room for at most two other cars, should anyone else wish to undertake this undoubtedly hazardous expedition. I think there were two daring groups of motorists on that brilliant summer day. It took a good deal of cosy hanging about while a few foot passengers ambled on to the platform with their shopping, and various odd packages were disposed of in convenient corners or around our bumpers. After everybody had satisfactorily bedded down, the engine had been coaxed into action, and we had chugged ponderously across to Kyleakin. Quite safely, as it turned out, sitting undisturbed in our open Morris Minor as we enjoyed the superb view.

In 1988 it was a little different. Everything was on a grander scale, the ferry now having an open deck on to which about twenty-five cars were obediently marshalled. Later ferries were another story: monstrous creatures into the dark bowels of which, rank on rank, we were cajoled and chivvied and hustled like a flock of wary sheep, and from which we disentangled ourselves, stumbling over iron bollards and up narrow stairways to a shuddering medley of benches and bars, upper decks and lower decks, snugly glazed look-outs and healthy open-air promenades. But it was just as exhilarating an adventure as it had been fifty years before, and we idled happily through Skye, discovered a little lost Celtic stone, squelched through the misty bogginess of the glorious Quirang, and eventually crossed the puffin-crested Minch from Uig to Tarbert in Harris.

And so to Lewis. In the end, we came to rest at what must be one of the most perfect bays in the world, in a hotel which is also one of the most delectable. It even offered, close by, the further all-this-and-heaven-too of a tiny graveyard from which, as legend has it, one of the great Highland foretellers, Coinneach Odhar, Dun Kenneth, known as the Brahan Seer, received from his mother the hollow stone through which he looked out at the future.

Legends are, of course, a great feature of both the past and the present of the Celtic world, and Callanish has its share: of the king-priest who came with other priests in robes of bird-skins and feathers to build their temple; of St Kiaran, arriving to preach Christianity to an ancient race of giants, but irritably turning them to stone when they refused to listen, having no doubt their own ideas on the matter. There is also the 'Shining One' who walks the stone avenue of Callanish, his coming announced by a cuckoo's cry from the isles of Tir-nan-Og, that paradise of youth now drowned beneath the sea. Yes, a place of mystery, the entrance into another world.

Stuffed full of those legends we came to Callanish, that Norse Kjallari-Ness as it may have been, a long, low ridge of trampled turf, patched here and there to heal the wounds made by tourist boots; a lonely country, not quite an island but jutting out into the quiet sea-waters of East Loch Roag. Strangely, the first impression one has is of seeing reality at two incongruous and separate levels. All around is a peat landscape, dotted with small, shacky croft houses and basic bungalows, giving an impression of rural inelegance, crude, unkempt, undistinguished, the ancient moor disturbed by a rather dreary muddle of boxes for living in. Yet, along that one isolated ridge hemmed in by placid water and distant hills, another world stands silently waiting: a long avenue of huge stones, a close-grouped circle, touched to a bright shining in the inter-mittent sunlight. The stones respond, as do the dolphins, to sun and cloud, one moment almost incandescent, as if about to dance, the next, inert and heavy, withdrawn into ambiguous and somewhat threatening retreat.

Seen from a distance, raised a little above the surrounding

peatland and silhouetted against the sky, the stones appear as a great company of people, taller and more substantial than we, grouped together companionably at the centre and occupied with their own affairs which are certainly not ours. It was some time after we returned home that I discovered they have long been known as the *Fir Bhreig*, the 'false men', but it did not need a legend to make such an obvious and overwhelming point. There they stood, existing in total detachment from the widespread, man-made clutter, untouched by today, alive within their own time, into which we may not venture. As you turn your head, you have the insistent feeling that you are catching the tail-end of movement; that the women gathered about the central menhir are about to change position, inter-mingling with each other. You take your intrusive photo-graphs (which did come out, so perhaps something was permitted), and these seem to confirm that sense of a stirring restlessness. How could *this* view possibly tie-up with *that*? They *must* have walked away. . . .

And immediately I felt my attitude towards distant Stonehenge had been vindicated. Nobody could imagine those massive southern trilithons stirring one single inch. Undoubtedly they were not meant to, and I thought that the people who had erected them must have been very limited in vision, concerned with suffocation and a hedging in of the spirit, in contrast with the builders of Callanish. Stonehenge is remarkable, within its powerful and regimented grouping of almost identical megaliths. But there is a sameness about all those enormously thick slabs which conveys a sense of individuality having been crushed: as if a gathering of clones was what had actually been required and eventually achieved. In the north, a colder, wilder habitat where the sheer business of keeping alive might have been expected to restrict imagination and intuition as well as craftsmanship, and where an infusion of ideas from the outside world would have been rare, we find, instead of those lumbering, weighted-down couples, a more delicately moulded creation, a company of separate and singular beings with their own authentic personalities. Each of the great stones of the Callanish avenue, though a part of the whole by reason of their substance and positioning, is in itself unique, fantastically shaped and grained, each seeming to strike a pose which is particular to itself, some even to bow their heads in acknowledgement of each other. I found myself amazed by the quality of life which almost cried out of the stones.

There were other visitors perching, alas, upon the grave slabs for happy snaps. Somehow that was shocking. But they went at last and would in any case have cast no ripple over the peaceful community. Only I, the edgy modern pilgrim, felt censorious, and who am I to take upon myself what the stones ignore? I wander among them, aware of my exclusion, knowing I cannot step across from our world into theirs, recognizing that I, in this place, am the alien. Even my childhood's admission card to 'stone-ness' offers no valid currency here. These are different beings from the smaller companions I had wept over as I buried them. Now, I have to tread delicately, my touch only fleeting.

I remembered the countless stories of 'merry maidens' turned to stone because they had danced on the Sabbath; of Old Meg and her daughters waiting for eternity; of the Rollright knights and their men, enchanted by a witch; of the stones which move, the stones which sing, the stones which fall upon those who seek to take them away. I remembered, too, those southern avenues of alternating male and female stones, so I looked about me and saw the large, full-bosomed authority of 'the Lady', the neater, smooth-capped efficiency of 'the Nurse', the group of slender, gracefully garbed women standing modestly and attentively about that essentially male figure towering above them all. I wondered what it would have meant and I thought it must have been about fertility and sacrifice, told through the symbolism of the dance ritual, though the victim would have been no symbol.

Living in those Stone and Bronze Age times, there would have been men and women, smaller and human, who would have erected those larger stone people and set up the long avenue of approach. Like the builders of Corrimony, they would have been no rough, crude savages with hair matted over frightened eyes and communicating in guttural grunts. They, too, would have rejoiced in the perfection of their handiwork, having a purpose in what they were doing which had taken them beyond themselves and the scratching up of poor grain to provide their unrewarding livelihood. Modern researchers into the still unknown, and perhaps unknowable, reasons behind the building of these vast stone circles have increasingly been obsessed with what is now called 'astro-archaeology' or the 'quest for the calendar'. Dazzling arguments are put forward but all too often, it seems to me, simple facts are being held enthusiastically – and with great learning – by investigators who turn a blind eye to those existing bits of information which do not fit. I find it difficult to agree with all the skilfully argued theories that late neolithic and Bronze Age people used their stone circles simply as gigantic observatories to determine the seasons and thus to establish some kind of calendar. So much is open to speculation as well as inaccuracy: the complicated mathematics of ascertaining, in relation to the stones, the actual star positions five thousand years ago; the problem that some stones will have fallen, only to be set up again in positions which may not have been theirs originally; the fact that in some of the circles, as at Callanish, the closeness of the central stone grouping would have made accurate readings unlikely.

There is also another argument against the quest for the calendar. In 3000 BC the landscape would have been well afforested. It seems to me that today's 'notch' on a distant horizon – to which certain stones are considered to be aligned, giving readings for a setting or rising sun or moon – might well have been filled to the brim with thick vegetation, while some intermediate hillock, now bare, might then have carried a dense growth of trees effectually blocking any sight of the 'notch'.

What the astro-archaeologists seem to have uncovered is the probability, almost the certainty, that the priest-guardians of the circles would have organized their building in such a way that they themselves could experiment intelligently in attempts to understand the movements of sun, moon and stars. These strange objects, so independent, so awesome, so rhythmic in their annual recurrences, must surely have appeared to the people of those early days as manifestations of their gods. It is likely, therefore, that any star studies undertaken with the aid of the circles may have been twofold in intention. At one level would have been the desire to manipulate sun or moon within the temple's religious rites. For instance, at Callanish we find two important stones placed outside the general plan, facing each other across the central circle and aligned to the northerly limit of the moon's eighteen-year cycle. Possibly this provides the first incontestable proof that ancient peoples searched the night sky and were aware of the patterns formed upon it. Indeed, what would we expect? What else had prehistoric people to look at to excite their wonder? They would surely have tried to read the heavens as we might read a book, in fear at times or in excited bewilderment, but a bewilderment which would change over thousands of years into familiarity with a nightly, monthly, yearly drama. Maybe, judging from those two odd men out at Callanish, this whole temple was dedicated to the moon goddess: the preponderance of female figures would also argue for this theory. But the mystery of the sun's transit of the heavens, and of the moon's crossing of the night sky, brings us to what must surely have been a rather different compulsion: the awakening of that fiery human quest after knowledge for its own sake, not simply to enhance the rituals of worship but to satisfy the passion of the mind. It would have been the same compulsion which drove Icarus: the need to explore, to go 'always a little further'.

As for the calendar, such matters would have been worked out, as various authorities have suggested, with simpler tools than the erection of enormous stone circles. Today, most of us have lost the ability to do without a printed diary of events, so that gardeners will say to each other: 'Easter next weekend. I'll be putting the tatties in.' In those earlier days they would have known the right moment for planting by the feel of the earth, crumbling it in their hands, treading it beneath their feet; by the way the light fell on a well-known piece of the landscape; by the touch of the wind, bringing once again the beginning of warmth. There would have been a few old men sitting in the sun, and one of them would have nodded towards a tree on the edge of the forest, saying: 'Notice how the sun's reached our tree at last? Time to get the seeds in.' And another old man would have wet his finger and held it up into the new, soft wind. 'Aye,' he would agree, 'and I felt the soil yesterday. It's ready.'

The stones would have been apart from such mundane matters. They would have been a temple, a meeting-place, a place of lawgiving, suitably massive and enduring, within which men and women (perhaps, at Callanish, the women?) would perform their religious rituals. For nearly five thousand years this vast structure has been standing, spread out along its low ridge and, though deeply scoured by weather, it is still overwhelming. But imagine what it was like when it was first erected, each stone meticulously shaped, pale and smooth and shining! Then, it would have been a miracle rising out of that dark landscape into the wide sky. Never surely a useful stone diary, but a holy place, to be entered with due trepidation and homage.

Looking about me as I moved around the circle, I felt sure that these people, having so carefully and with precise structural knowledge, built their temple, would then have danced in procession along that great avenue, weaving

among the two lines of megaliths and mingling at the
centre with the stone men and women they had raised up;
even, it may have been implanting their released energies
into the receptive stones to form a barrier against the
intrusion of unwelcome spirits. At some of the circles, as
with the Rollright Stones in Oxfordshire, a rhythmic
pulsing has been instrumentally recorded, deep within the
stones and emitted by them as if they were some kind of
dynamo still retaining and storing the mental 'push' of
intense emotional and religious fervour. These recordings
may or may not have led to an accurate interpretation of
the phenomenon, but certainly the findings are curious.
And up here, in this northern outpost of mankind, you
cannot help but sense how strong would have been the
impulsion of fear or supplication, of dread or anger, horror
or pity, as the people of that desolate region danced their
rituals to placate their gods.

Callanish is a strange place, perhaps the strangest of all
those ancient groups of standing stones. It is so old, so
remote. And the things that once happened there are still
embedded within it. The stones lead their own contained
existence, indifferent to anything around them. Not
gentle, no. Even, in a curious way, inimical. They are
caught within their whole long history of time past, that
'constancy of time' from which we have moved all too fast.
As I, the intruder, walk among them, I am increasingly
aware of their almost movement, of a leaning forward, the
beginning of a carefully constructed dance. For a fraction
of time it seems about to begin. But my too too solid flesh
prevents understanding. And the glimpse, like the flick of a
shutter, is lost. But, left to themselves, the stones are
poised and ready.

The child I once had been would have used her admission
card to stone-ness for a deeper perception of Callanish
than I could hope to achieve. That child had once, on a
never to be forgotten occasion, attended the old Diaghilev
Russian Ballet at a performance of Bakst's *Sleeping Princess*

when the great classical dancers of a now long-vanished world had brought to life the fairy-tale in which she herself was spending her own sleeping youth. She would have understood about the awakening of the stones' frozen movement; would have eagerly watched for some miracle, a rising of the curtain on a drama staged in a long-ago past. At the same time she would have known, thankfully, that it could not happen. But I was not that child. I could not any longer enter her unfenced world. I could only use my imagination to understand what Callanish would once have been. Yet I could see, as she would have seen, that whatever of horror might have chilled the blood in certain of the rituals, above all it would have been a place of astounding beauty, the triumphant creation of a people deprived of everything the modern world holds dear, but who were able, having only their hands to work with, to translate their inner vision into enduring stone.

The oldest part of Callanish was built about 3000 BC: that slender central menhir which rises almost to sixteen feet, and the surrounding circle stones, together with the little stone cairn which lies immediately in front of the menhir and was used for cremation burials. Until recently the cairn was thought to have been added a century or so later, but modern analysis has dated it more precisely. Pot fragments have also been found, dating back to about 2000–1700 BC, so that the whole area was in use throughout the later neolithic period and into about the middle of the Bronze Age. But there are uncertainties and differences of opinion about the dating, especially over the erection of the avenue. Much later, the whole semi-island returned to the original farming use which, in a milder climate than that of today, had led to the cultivation of cereals. Still later, peat began to cover the long ridge of Callanish and by the nineteenth century had reached a depth of five feet, as if to swallow the stones back into the primeval rock. This was cleared away in 1957.

But to look back a mere five thousand years is to ignore

the vast age of the stones themselves. They were hewn by neolithic men from Lewisian gneiss, some of the oldest rock in the world, having been laid down about 2,600 million years ago. This is found mainly on the Isle of Lewis and the Inner Hebrides, as also on the opposite mainland where, in Sutherland, the Torridon sandstone peaks of Cul Beag, Stac Pollaidh, Cul Mor, Canisp, Suilvan, Quinag and Ben Stac rise up in a magnificent mountain chain from their roots in Lewisian gneiss. Some of the surface rocks on Lewis are the remains of ancient mountains that would have been similar but are long since eroded.

Lewisian gneiss is a metamorphic rock – that is, one which has changed its structure. This came about as a result of the pressure and heat generated by the tremendous bending and breaking movements of the earth's crust when the great mountain ranges were being thrown up. It is wonderfully formed of quartz, feldspar, mica and hornblende, in a most extraordinary mixture, being ridged and banded into rippling waves of contorted and heavily compressed patterns. Looking at the avenue stones, you are seeing massive individual pieces of rock, yet they all have a deceptive appearance of being grained like wood. Photography often reveals this very clearly: with the sun at a low angle, the knots and rings as of a tree are sharply delineated and for a moment, as you glance along the line of stones, you almost believe you are seeing the great trunks of an ancient forest. The circle, too, is grained in such a way that some of the stones appear to be shrouded in pleated scarves and drifting skirts, the clothing petrified along with the people.

In walking around Lewis we tread upon this most ancient rock as it pokes through the skin of soil or peat. The standing stones, artificially cut from reasonably accessible quarries and then up-ended, are part of that earth foundation of 2,600 million years. But although I scramble so casually over the stony hillsides of Lewis, I know quite well that, if one of the stones of Callanish were to have fallen to the ground, I would carefully walk round it. Nothing would induce me either to defile or to provoke it.

We drove away reluctantly, stopping every now and then to look back. Across the rolling peatland we could still see that distant ridge where, as it chanced, the stones shone pale gold in the sun; no longer heavy rock but transmuted into thin, cold flames that flickered along the horizon. The tall group at the centre shifted continually as the angle of vision changed. The avenue streamed away towards the north. I felt that nothing could intrude upon them, that they existed in some other dimension of reality. For a fraction of time we had walked among them, though without what could be called an encounter, and now, in leaving the place where they had stood for so many ages, we were returning to our own reality of the twentieth century. They remained, and always would remain, untouched by our transient interest. I felt a sense of relief that this should be so.

After I had left Callanish I was to find that its impact would increase rather than diminish. Seemingly it has the capacity to keep hold of you and to reveal more of itself, piece by piece, in sudden enlightenment. Sometimes I find myself looking out of the window at home and thinking, Why, yes, that must have been what happened! Why didn't I think of it at the time? But 'at the time' was too much and too many. It all took quite a while to settle down inside me.

One result of this has been a heightened awareness not only of the stones but of the people who raised them. Every one of us alive today has come from and is part of a fragile, stretched-out line of men and women reaching back to even earlier days than those of the bronze workers or the builders with stone. Conditions for the origin of many of us would have been determined according to the warmth or coldness, fertility or impoverishment, of our own part of the earth's surface. But for all of us there would have been, at the far distant beginning of that thread of life, those forerunners who eventually became a handful of hunting people, pitting their wits against an overwhelming natural environment, ever moving on and moving on. In our northern lands, a sparse sprinkling of these roving families would have encountered each other, spread thinly over endless swamp and forest land. And at last, some of them having become settled farmers, they would have joined together, in lives of fearful deprivation as judged by modern standards, to build stone cairns and circles: witness to their emerging ideas and beliefs, to the untutored searching of their minds, to their longing for something beyond their own small, finite selves.

Tiny particles of those far-off men and women are miraculously lodged within the genetic structure of each one of us, transmitted along those frail but persistent lines of descent. We have come out of, and still belong to, the vast loneliness and tenacity of those distant peoples.

— 10 —

The Hermit's Cave

Although I am isolated from all other buildings on my cliff-top, this does not mean no people come up and down the track or along the cliff. They arrive by car, by moped, by bicycle or come on foot, not necessarily to see either me or Halley, and falling mainly into three categories. There are the summer tourists, some of whom camp near the lighthouse with a clutch of infants, who totter bravely through the nettles. Their aim is vaguely to walk 'away there to the castle', which they can see sticking up as a gaunt ruin in the far distance. Noting the small fry, I shake my head gloomily, pointing out that there is no path beyond the next few hundred yards; that the coast thereafter is exceedingly rough; that it will take much longer to get there than they think, and that – naturally – it is just beginning to rain. Human nature being what it is, this usually confirms the leader of the expedition in his determination to proceed at all costs, undaunted by the woebegone children in their unsuitable sandals and thin T-shirts, or by the harassed mother who obviously views the whole enterprise with despair.

However, I am comfortably certain that all will be well and do not feel too worried as they struggle southward along what becomes an increasingly inaccessible cliff-top. When eventually the safari reaches the end of the path, with no way forward and only the dismal return being apparent, it comes to an abrupt halt and the entire family vanishes from sight as if precipitated down a crevasse.

Which is just what has happened. By this I know that they have found the steep way to the shore, which will offer a pleasant meander back to the lighthouse car-park. The mother will have given thanks for such an unexpected deliverance; the father will have saved face as he plunges forward on this new and more rewarding exploration; the children will have run shrieking to the water's edge and with luck will manage not to break their little legs by slipping on the wet rocks.

Other visitors are more prepared. There are the winkle-pickers. Nothing to do with the one-time popular footwear, but unemployed families seeking to turn an honest penny by harvesting a sack or two of seafood, and hoping they are far enough from home not to be recognized by the powers that be. Invariably they park their cars alongside the coastguard house – some of them even asking if they may! – and depart down the cliff, laden with sacks and buckets and preceded by small tribes of offspring. Little fingers, as the cotton millers were aware, are ideal for any finicky task such as detaching reluctant winkles from a wet rock. And certainly it is agonizing work, the shore soaked from the receding tide, the fingers, both large and small, becoming numbed and yellow, the eyes stung by an often searing wind. They deserve all they can earn, especially since, after perhaps five or six hours, they have then to hump the sodden sacks up an uncooperative cliff.

A third category is composed of the 'odd bods', those who may appear occasionally: fishermen in search of a variety of coloured floats, drifted ashore and now entangled at the edge of the rocks; enthusiasts with CB radios, chatting to their chums across the water; earnest young students fossil-hunting or doing a night recording of seal voices; Range-Rovers, again with night-comers, searchlighting the cliff for foxes, though not with any particularly friendly intentions; the bird expert, surrounded by his acolytes, being lowered on a much-used rope down the sheerer rock-faces in the pitch dark of night to ring protesting fulmars.

Not many passers-by are actual visitors, though one of them would very much have liked to be. It happened shortly after I had moved in, and I was down on the shore, dancing. This perhaps needs a little explanation, since it had nothing to do with either classical ballet or modern dance rhythm. An onlooker would not have thought for a moment that the gumbooted, anoraked, woolly hatted female lurching around at the edge of the sea was doing anything of the kind. But she was – or at any rate in her mind. It was all so new and beautiful: the soft green shore, the glittery pools, the frothy waves breaking peacefully over those strangely fashioned rocks. So I danced. Throwing my arms wide and flapping up and down in the beginnings of flight, singing my own orchestral accompaniment, clumping up and down as the incoming tide swished around my boots. It never occurred to me that I might be observed. The shore looked so deserted. But I should have remembered that whenever anybody believes themselves to be alone, there is bound to be an avidly curious head popping up behind a hedge. For me, as I turned at length and began a more sober walk towards the cliff, it was an exceedingly interested man, reclining comfortably in the shelter of a whin-bush and waving a large bottle at me. There seemed to be another bottle, empty, upturned at his feet. So I hurried past, with what dignity I could muster, keeping as much distance between us as possible and ignoring his unintelligible but clearly enthusiastic invitations.

About half an hour later, when I was safely restored to the house, there came a pounding at the back door. When I opened it, he was there, now minus both bottles and swaying gracefully to and fro.

'C'n I c'min?' This with a fuzzy leer.

'No!' I replied stiffly, remembering all those dire warnings to women who live by themselves in solitude.

He gazed at me wistfully. 'Carn I c'min?'

'Certainly not.' I spoke austerely, hoping to blot out his

probable vision of our dancing together round the kitchen
table. '*Certainly* not,' I repeated emphatically and shut the
door.

It took some time before his rejection got through to
him, so I hid discreetly in a corner and watched until at last
he wandered off towards the front gate and the track to the
road. But there came an unexpected end to the affair. It
was early days at the house on the cliff and my landlords
had been busy taking away the broken garden fence, with
the intention of renewing it. The gate itself, a large and
rather handsome structure, was still standing but without
being attached to anything. It simply offered the rather
surrealistic scene of a gate all by itself in the middle of
nowhere. This, however, was not what my bottle-fed
intruder was seeing. Without any question he had been
curtly dismissed, and when that happens you exit politely
by the front gate. This he attempted to do, as any well-bred
gentleman might. Unfortunately the gate had a peculiar
latch, which has foxed many a visitor. It took him a
considerable time to discover how it worked.

I watched, entranced. But the penny never dropped, and
he remained totally unaware that he had only to walk
around the side of the gate and, hey presto, the world was
his. Instead, it took him at least five minutes concentrated
fiddling before, with absorbed determination, he found the
secret and stumbled down the step. After which he spent
another five minutes courteously fastening it up again, and
then swept off with great dignity – if also a pronounced
wobble. But he had vindicated his good manners, and I was
left wiping the tears from my eyes.

Some other visitors, though of a different kind, caused
me acute anxiety. There is always the lone winkler,
disappearing down the cliff into a thick fog, to work his
way along the slippery rocks. The tide will be going out and
he will follow it. But the hours go by and presently the tide
will be returning, quietly determined. Also the fog has
thickened and the short day darkened and the empty car is

still waiting beside the house. It is then that I start fidgeting, my imagination seeing him trapped in a deep pool with a broken leg and the waves licking at his boots. When there is a companion, I never bother, since it would be stretching probability too far to conceive that both have been incapacitated at the same time. But the loner is always, alas, the one who knows best. He it is who, never having been along our coast before, is convinced that he is invulnerable. So I give a short, sharp sigh, gaze longingly at the glowing fire and the curled-up Halley, pull on my gumboots, bad-weather helmet, anorak, scarf, gloves, binoculars and then begin plodding along the edge of the cliff in the hope of spotting my quarry and, having satisfied myself that he is in no difficulty, beat a tactful retreat. Sometimes I go out two or three times, searching for a tell-tale yellow or scarlet plastic bucket wedged into the rocks. Once I was utterly defeated and, after six or seven hours had passed, was on the point of ringing the coastguard, when I made out a burdened figure staggering back towards the car, having come up the cliff nearly a mile from where he had started.

There was another loner, too, but he was undoubtedly what might be termed the precipitating factor in my own adventure with the hermit's cave. He was a wildly enthusiastic young man, dedicated, quite impossibly, to restoring the remains of a small building about a mile south along the shore, which he insisted had been a hermit's cell. Only the foundations remained and, since there was no access road of any kind, and since he was married with several small children, the project was clearly doomed from the start. Still, I could appreciate his infatuation, though even I could not share it. He went off, one dreary afternoon, to survey the 'property', and I just managed to keep his attention sufficiently fixed on the deteriorating state of the weather, so that he understood, if only vaguely, that once at the bottom of the cliff, he would have to take a long, cool look at its structure. This was because on his return journey he needed to recognize that particular place, among a lot of almost identical rocky outcrops, as the point at which the cliff path began its ascent. But of course, though he acknowledged me, it was wasted effort. I could see him busily forgetting the advice even as he turned away. Hours later he came in sight from the opposite direction, having entirely failed to recognize anything at all. He had then tramped endlessly along the shore, through mud and rain, until almost reaching the lighthouse, when he had surfaced on to the cliff to begin his forlorn trek back. Thereafter he came once or twice, but eventually he abandoned his project. It was on that earlier occasion, seeing him so draggled, that I gave my classic admonition, which was to come in handy on so many similar occasions: 'You know, this is *not* a "fun" coast!'

Indeed it is not. Summer visitors, lulled to complacency by a glittering sea and a gentle, whin-golden cliff, imagine it to be a kindly terrain. However, in winter (or in summer, come to that), with the landmarks blotted out by haar, it can be alarming and even hostile. As I was to find out. For, although I felt sure that the hermit's 'cell' was only the remains of a shore-line bothy, possibly used at one time for storing fishing-tackle, I knew that there was indeed a hermit's cave tucked away at the foot of a scooped-out cliff and facing down a steep slope of raised beach. It would be nice to find it, to pay my respects to that other seeker after solitude who must surely have found even more than he would have bargained for than I had, back in the less cultivated wildness to which, in some early Christian century, he had removed himself.

Yet even as my enthusiasm mounted, and as I tried to pinpoint the exact location on a local map, I began to have a few qualms. The cave was outside what I always thought of as 'our' territory, which means another area of farmland and cliff. That shore, rarely grazed by sheep, was therefore deep in thistles and nettles and rough grass, all swamping a scattering of rocks and the remains of more modern impedimenta in the shape of abandoned refrigerators and even an old car – presumably tipped over the cliff at one stage of its decline. But it was not so much the obstacles, natural or mechanical, which worried me, as the strong feeling of aversion I had always felt when wandering in that direction; almost of warning, as if a small dark cloud had settled there, definitely inimical and telling me that beyond the fence any such hermit's cave would prove to be unfriendly. Nothing more positive, only this scarcely perceptible atmosphere, a sense of needing to be wary, of reluctance to venture along what was in any case an even more deserted shore than my own.

I was only too well aware that I attributed my uneasiness to the hermit who had once lived there, as if he were still active, surrounded by a large 'keep-out' aura. Yet I told myself I was being stupid. He had lived, if indeed he ever had lived, many centuries ago. He had been dead a long time. And he could have been a lovely old man, probably resembling St Francis, and someone who had long chats with sea-gulls. His cave might even have been populated with stoats and weasels, all devotedly ministering to his needs. On the other hand, he could have been a misogynistic, cantankerous old busybody, hating everyone and looking out of his cave with loathing, were another human being to venture near. It's often difficult to tell, with people who seek isolation.

But I was determined to reconnoitre, so I set forth one morning, making my way rapidly down the cliff path, turning right at the bottom and proceeding with a glow of anticipation along the level, sheep-cropped grass, with its patches of pinkish thrift bordering the sea. It was a golden day, offering a rare promise of extreme heat. The gulls were nesting among the litter of stones beside the shore, slapdash collections of twigs and other muddle dropped casually into any old corner – though never below the high-water mark. After a while I arrived at the broken-down stretch of wire fencing which marked the boundary,

finding a different kind of nest wedged into a rocky cleft,
which contained one large, almost round, plain, green-blue
egg. No birds were within sight. Perhaps, I thought, I had
driven them away. Perhaps the egg was there to distract
me from what I was about to do. But, I asked myself, *what*
was I about to do? Only to climb over, fight my way around
the abandoned, rusting car and struggle up the perhaps
thirty-degree slope to the foot of that recessed cliff. There,
to take a look inside what might remain of this hermit's
cave. Only to take a look, not to go in. Certainly not. I had
never cared much for confined spaces.

It was a tiresome ascent, even though not more than a
couple of hundred yards. To start with, the nettles were
almost head high and what grass there was now grew in
huge clumps, each one cunningly protecting a half-hidden
boulder, which I discovered only when I had tripped over it.
There were sudden gullies, too, open-jawed to trap my
gumboots. Fortunately gumboots give excellent ankle
support, which is why I prefer them to ordinary climbing
boots. But I wished I had brought a stick. I wished it had not
turned out to be so hot. There were flies. Also . . . also I did
not like the place.

What had I always been called? Stubborn. Obstinate. Pig-
headed. So I went ahead, determined to find the cave.
When I got there, I found myself standing beneath an
overhang of the sandstone cliff. Obviously pieces of the
cliff-face had frequently fallen, lying now among the
nettles in a jumble of enormous, sharp-edged chunks. I
edged my way round them, finding a long slit at the bottom
of the cliff, narrow, like a mouth half opening. There were
only a few feet of negotiable entry, and I could see that the
shallow cave ran back in a steep, downward slope.
Centuries of rubble and ground-up sandstone had accumu-
lated until there was never more than about six feet from
floor to roof. It did not look inviting.

I stood there for a long time, peering in, feeling curiously
light and disembodied, unable to make a decision. Well, I'd

got here, hadn't I? At long last I had discovered the place. No need to go any further. Just a rather grimy little cave, getting narrower and narrower as it thrust its way into the base of the cliff. Absolutely nothing to be seen. Nothing to be felt, either. No auras. No emanations. Somebody, not so long ago, had been here before me, and remarks had been scratched – but only on the outside – of the 'I was here' variety. But had the hermit himself ever been here? And if not, why had I always felt uncomfortable about that particular piece of shore? I thought I might just clamber down inside and take a look around. There could be some indication of his tenancy. After all, I had come a long way. Silly to turn back without actually having explored the place.

Still I hesitated, then, pulling myself together, I took the first step towards that shelving entrance, catching hold of its upper lip for support and beginning to lower myself inside. And immediately I slipped. Being on a slope, my feet shot out before me and I crashed down heavily on to my back, landing with extreme force upon the sharp point of a jutting rock.

I was not stunned. I did not faint. Nor was I even winded. But I knew at once that I was damaged. So I lay there, not attempting to move, the rock feeling as if it were embedded into my lower spine and my feet more or less inside the cave and up in the air. You are, I said wearily to myself, you *are* a damn fool.

But of course I had to get up, so, after warily testing what parts of my anatomy I could reach, I began to roll slowly over, levering myself into a useful position for getting to my feet. And for the first few seconds I thought, with a gasping rush of relief, that it was all right, that I was only shaken. Until, pulling myself upright against the face of the rock, and half turning away from the cave, I was suddenly convulsed with pain. It was like nothing I had ever known, a rending flash which left me sick and whimpering. Though, even in the middle of it, I was telling myself that it was *not* my spine and *not* my hip joint but another less crucial place somewhere in between. Trying to sit down, I found I couldn't, and when I put a foot forward, the pain flooded through me again. But I found it was not constant, coming when I got myself into a position it did not care for. Hanging on to the rock which, having carried out its task, was now all helpful crevices for my groping fingers, I began to edge my way to the top of the raised beach. I looked down at my gumboots, those good, true friends which, in all my scrambling over wet rocks, had never let me down. No, it was not their fault.

Eventually I stood free of the cave, out in the hot sun. I found I was shaking all over and that with every slicing of pain I was reduced to a sick sweat. I also felt that I could, though I must not, quite easily faint. But I was well aware that somehow I must get myself home. I took a quick look towards the boundary fence in the faint hope that the sheep might be on our shore, which would mean that my shepherd friend would eventually come this way. But of course they were down on the Dornoch side. So, no rescue party. And absolutely no chance of making anybody hear my cries. I considered this with rising panic, knowing it might be days or even weeks before the sheep came back. And days or weeks were what I had not got. I certainly did not wish to become a small heap of bones for whoever happened, much later, to come along. I had no illusions about sea-gulls.

It was here that my not very endearing traits of obstinacy and pig-headedness showed their beneficial aspect. I am, I told myself with total, unyielding determination, going home – now, this minute. In a way, the worst bit was those two hundred yards of raised beach, sloping down at such a steep angle among the many hidden pitfalls. I also knew that even when, or if, I reached the bottom, and even if I managed to negotiate the comparatively flat shore, I would then have the cliff to climb. Well, one thing at a time, I decided. Let's got on with it. So I started off, very gingerly, every single step of that boulder-strewn descent sending a sheet of pain through the small of my back. It took a long time before I ended up against the blessed haven of the dilapidated old car, and I clung to it with tears of exhaustion and relief. At least the car, rearing up on its shattered side, gave me shade from the sun, so I rested, if not happily then gratefully against its crumpled wing before tackling the fence. Here I remember looking for the green-blue egg, only to find it was no longer there. I remember, too, that I was puzzled – extravagantly puzzled, considering the circumstances – over its disappearance, staring and staring in disbelief. Perhaps a black-backed gull had demolished it. But there were no fragments of shell. Or perhaps, I wondered dizzily, there never had been an egg, just a lure to lead me on.

Having eased myself through a tangled gap in the fence, I found that by dint of edging forward crabwise, taking tiny steps, one behind the other in a kind of shuffle, I could do something to avoid the worst of the jabs, so that, although the shore seemed to stretch away for miles, I got myself along it reasonably well. The cliff was another matter, since I could not begin to walk up it. I gazed with the beginning of despair at the precipitous track, twisting perilously near the edge of several overhangs and criss-crossed with roots of whin. No problem if you were stumping your way up it after a peaceful morning collecting bits of driftwood, with nothing deeper to exercise your mind or body but the growing desire for a cup of coffee. But now? It could have been Everest for all the accessibility it offered. Still, the simple fact remained: I had to get up it.

So I got down on my hands and knees, finding to my surprise a sudden relief from pain, and began the intermi-nable ascent, clinging on to the prickly whin-bushes and grappling them to me as one is supposed to grapple one's trusty friends, though my arms by then were hardly hoops of steel. Again, it all took a long time. And the creature who eventually got to the top and inched her way along the last little stretch and over the stile and across the garden, was certainly not that jaunty adventurer who had started out so blithely a few hours earlier. After I had got myself inside the house, everything became a little blurred. I remember I telephoned the doctor. I remember drinking a strong brandy, my teeth chattering with reaction. And then, somehow, I rolled on to the bed, an act which immediately convulsed me in waves of pain. But it did not matter any more. All I had to do was to huddle there, thankfully to await the arrival of our never-sufficiently-to-be-praised health service. I had made it. Stubbornness had paid off.

Recovery from what seemed to have been a damaged ligament took a long time, during which I did a lot of hard thinking. Partly my thoughts were of my own idiocy and how it was no use telling strong, active, young men, reprovingly, that this was not a 'fun' coast, when I had not even the sense to look after myself. But also my thoughts were of the cave and the hermit and the oddness of what had happened. I knew that I was never casual in my cliff wanderings, aware always of the need to watch my step in such rough country. Nor was I accident prone, rather priding myself on being reasonably sure-footed. But it had happened, and I did not like it. I had felt for years that there was something unlucky about that patch of cliff and now I was certain of it. There was a darkness there, and though I did not want to become involved – had already been far too dangerously close – I knew that, in a queer way, an obligation had been laid upon me; that I was now responsible for doing something about it. Doing what? There was nothing anybody could do. Yet the worry remained within me, an irritation which would not go away. In the end, reluctantly, I decided to take the only possible action to – what? Combat it? No, but perhaps to cancel it.

The decision brought an end to my restlessness and, many weeks later, on my first sortie down to the shore, I made myself go back, albeit slowly and with a stick. I did not cross the boundary, having no intention of going anywhere near the actual mouth of that cave ever again. But I went as close as I felt able, standing by the fence and looking up at the jumble of boulders and nettles to where, just out of sight, the cave entrance lay hidden behind the rock which had almost perforated me. I stood there for a long time, thinking about the hermit. Not a dear old man living delightfully with tame sea-gulls and lots of beautifully mannered stoats. No. Rather more of the other image: old and querulous and full of malice. And therefore a sad old man, suffering in his sour rejection of people, injuring himself by his implacable withdrawal and fanatical cursings. For cursings there must surely have been, since they appeared still to be operative, the hermit being unable to free himself from them even though he had been dead for several hundred years.

I was not at all sure what I had to do, never having witnessed any of the various forms of exorcism, though I had had a great deal to do with people who were mentally ill. But this was different. I was sure it was exorcism that was needed, and that I had no power to accomplish it myself. There were, I knew, certain prayers for the restraint of evil, certain rites available to certain people. But I was not one of them. I had no knowledge of what was said or done. So I thought that I must be as short, as concentrated, as direct, and as simple as it was possible to be.

In the end, I tried to empty myself of my own will, my own self-awareness, so that there was only, within me, a petition: asking, for the hermit, that his darkness – his demons? – should depart from him and never molest him again; asking that, within himself, he might find reconciliation; asking that he might shed his burden, whatever it had been. 'Into thy hands', I said aloud, meaning God's, 'I commend his spirit.' And, 'Into God's hands', I said to the long-dead hermit, 'I commend thy spirit.' And finally, using the old, familiar words: 'Grant him, O Lord, eternal rest. And let light perpetual shine upon him.' I made a careful sign of the cross towards the cave, since he would have been an old man who had endured suffering, adding: '*Requiescat in pace*.'

I waited a little while, trusting that perhaps he might have found a morsel of tranquillity. Then I went away. I have never been back to that part of the shore, so I do not know whether the cloud of his anger has gone.

11

No Abiding Place

The Dornoch shore, which I call the 'other side', is entirely different from my own cliff-top. To start with, there are no cliffs, only a few terraces of rough grass and whin shelving to the rocks from a long, flattish stretch of grazing land. In sunlight it is a glittering seascape of blue water, yellow rocks, bright green grass and almost sparkling, honey-scented whin. It is not wild at all, but a lovely, shining shore with many small coves cutting in among the rocks, these being much in demand in the old days as conveniently secret landing-places for many a smuggler. In fact the imprint of humans is another distinguishing mark, and even to look at the map reveals how, from prehistoric times, incomers settled on that 'other side' in preference to traipsing up and down steep cliffs. There are groups of ancient cairns and kitchen middens, which may be neolithic but are now buried deep beneath the unevenly humped grass; though one enormous solitary boulder remains of what could have been a Bronze Age structure. There is also the completely overgrown mound of a ruined castle which stands high on a crag above a narrow rocky harbour, the inlet now marked on the map as *Port a' Chaisteil*. Yellow whin blooms above the flat, grass rampart of the *chaisteil*, but apart from this walkway there is little to suggest the mound is different from the other crags that border the shore.

However, something a bit more historical emerges from the grazing land above the jumble of rocks. On the map it is

Blar a' Chath, the field of the battle, and this is not surprising, since Norse invaders and Scottish (or Pictish) peoples were constantly at war with each other from the ninth to the twelfth centuries AD. It is generally accepted, and mentioned in one of the Norse sagas, that a great battle took place on 'Torfness' in which Thorfinn the Mighty, Earl of Orkney, was victorious over the ruler of Moray, also known as 'a king of the Scots' and thought of by some as possibly being the equally mighty Macbeth. This of course does present certain difficulties, since other authorities believe both these warriors to have been one and the same person. But there is only one *Blar a' Chath* marked on the maps of Tarbat Ness, so it is not just speculation to suggest that this is the site of that Torfness battle. Certainly, in the nineteenth century, various objects were found, such as an ancient sword and a bronze crucifix, probably brought to the surface during ploughing.

It is a shore that has been much lived in and fought over, but perhaps the most puzzling discovery is down on the actual rocks where curious upthrusts are to be found which seem to be volcanic in origin: double rows of thin, rusty-looking rock sticking up on end, sometimes a foot high. They run in absolutely straight avenues against the grain of the rocks, cutting across whatever angles these are lying at, and disappearing far out to sea. It is an extremely odd formation which I have never found on the Moray shore.

As I make my way beyond all these evidences of the past, it is the far Sutherland shore which holds me, that land which is north for all of us in the British Isles but a 'southland' for the invading Vikings. Down by the water and about a mile distant from each other are two buildings, both of them soaked in history though divided in time by about a thousand years. One of these is an ancient broch, the other, south-westward, is Dunrobin Castle. No two buildings could possibly be more unlike each other, yet in a curious way their beginnings had everything in common, since both were created as fortifications by the people who, in each period, were the most flourishing farmers of that countryside. Dunrobin, begun in the thirteenth century, is now almost wholly of the nineteenth century. The date of the broch is less certain and until recently would have been thought to fall somewhere within 100 BC and AD 100, and therefore to have been influenced by the threat of Roman invasion, by Iron Age settlers, and by the generally fluctuating movements of various refugee peoples. But Scottish prehistory is being revised almost every week. A short time ago it was thought possible that the brochs could be as ancient as 600 BC and as late as AD 200; now it is being pushed even further back, with suggestions of 800 BC. As one authority puts it: 'Everything is in a state of being worked over.'

If I say that the brochs of Scotland are out of this world, this is literally so, since in no other country can such buildings be found. They are unique. And they are beautiful: great concave towers of dry-stone walling, looking to the modern visitor like a rather smaller version of our own familiar and equally beautiful cooling towers. But very few now stand to their full height, and certainly no other broch will present such a remarkable spectacle as the famous Broch of Mousa in Shetland, which still rises some forty-three feet. Scotland is thick with the remains of these fortifications. There are more than five hundred of them, mostly clumped together in the far north-east up to Orkney and Shetland, with another dense grouping on the Isle of Skye, where some authorities believe they originated. Many are completely ruined and overgrown, never having been excavated. But there are still brochs which are wonderful to explore, the very best being those which stand far from later human settlements, thus escaping enthusiastic demolition for building material; also those not so close to the sea as to suffer from soil erosion, the fate of a good many, since the edge of the shore is a favourite place.

I look affectionately across the water at 'our' broch, appropriated because it is our nearest and is the place to which I take all my summer visitors. This means, until the new bridge over the Dornoch Firth is completed, a long trek round the head of the waters at Bonar Bridge. But the broch is well worth it. Many of the more important brochs are named, and ours is *Carn Liath*. Confusingly, this commonly appears on the maps for a number of quite dissimilar structures, any of which might answer to being a 'heap of grey stones'. The Gaelic *carn* is Anglicized as 'cairn' and often applied to round, rocky hills, some of the now toppled brochs having that appearance. *Liath*, pronounced without the last two letters so as to sound like the king, means 'grey'. But the general term of 'broch', coming from the old Norse *borg*, denotes a strong or fortified place, which conveys the real use of the towers.

But in spite of its name the Carn Liath Broch, though standing on rising ground, and certainly with its cooling-tower walls very much crumbled, has not in any way become just a 'heap of grey stones'. The interior was cleared in the nineteenth century, revealing the inner walling which rises to about twelve feet, and the whole place was tidied up in 1972. In its heyday it would have been a tall, windowless, circular tower, each stone carefully shaped and graded to fit precisely against its adjacent ones. And there is not just one wall: the secret of broch building is a double structure with an inner concentric wall exactly corresponding to the outer and having a space in between for a stone staircase leading to the top, with various galleries looking over the open space within the broch. The lower part of Carn Liath's staircase is still there, and, importantly for archaeologists, so is the narrow, east-facing entrance passage which is still lintelled with enormous flat stones. There would have been a massive wooden door, the only possible point of entry, with stone door-checks which still exist, and a bar-hole where we can see that a wooden cross-piece once rested. Also, within the two walls, there are the remains of a guard-cell. Had you wished to force your way in, there would definitely have been problems.

Inside the entrance, and past the guard-cell, you emerge into a grassy, open courtyard. The top of the broken wall has been turfed and you can walk round it, having ascended the staircase, and look down into what was the living area of the farmer who had ordered it to be built. Long ago there would have been a circle of timbered huts built with their backs to the wall. Outside the broch are the remains of small outbuildings, now being excavated, and possibly having been in use in more peaceful times when it was safe to live near but not necessarily within the broch. Even so, these huts were hedged around by an outer wall, the line of which is still to be seen.

From all this we can judge that Carn Liath, as all the brochs, would have been impregnable. At the approach of an enemy, people and cattle would have been crammed inside and the huge wooden door secured against the stone jambs. Everyone, including the beasts, would, though crowded, have managed reasonably well until the raiders had departed, which it seems they usually did fairly rapidly. There are few traces of weapons having been found in excavated brochs, probably because attackers, if unable to surprise the inhabitants before they could get themselves inside, would have known the enterprise to be hopeless. Further to discourage them, there would have been a kind of catwalk along the rim at the top, and this, as well as acting as a look-out post, would have come in handy for dropping a few rocks on to the frustrated foe.

The walls, being hollow, enabled the builders to ignore the problem of weight when thrusting the tower so high, and the brochs were the most advanced architecture of their time. Previously, small, low stone fortresses would have been used, and when the idea of broch building caught on, so that the more wealthy farmers vied with each other to erect bigger and better ones, it must have been an amazing sight for the ordinary people to watch these

cooling towers mounting skyward. Just as in our own day,
there might have been some who were all for a cranky new
architectural design, while others would have yearned
after a more old-fashioned style, grumbling to each other,
forming protest groups, getting up petitions, staging
demos, and arguing bitterly that the brochs spoilt the
skyline.

Most of the household goods unearthed in broch
excavation have been plain pottery vessels and tools made
of bone, such as wool-carding combs. But some of the
brochs have yielded delightful painted pebbles, either
charms or for use in games. These are decorated with
simple, sometimes abstract designs and look just as if they
had come from a modern craft-shop. The same patterns are
in use: a nice round, flat pebble was found having a painted
X upon it, with a neat round dot placed between each arm
of the X. It can be seen on endless picture postcard borders,
cups and saucers, curtaining materials, wall paper and
cushion covers of the twentieth century.

When I wander around Carn Liath I feel it is a
comfortable place, warm and lived in. It has no eerie, other-
world emanations, no hint of esoteric rites. It sits stockily
on its hump of land, well back from the Firth but facing
down the smooth sweep of land which ends today in a strip
of whin and then black rocks and the sea. Had I lived in it
when it was first built, my nearest neighbouring broch
would have been about two and a half miles away, along
what is now Dunrobin Glen. There would have been
another, just less than three miles to the north, and yet
another, now called Craig Carril, about a mile further on,
both of them on the Brora River. However, the Brora
River would not have existed under that name, and Craig
Carril would also have been called something different – if
it had had a name at all. North-eastward along the coast I
should have had to walk about seven miles or more before
reaching my next broch neighbour at Kintradwell, and it
would have been a much longer journey to the brochs of

the River Helmsdale. Going still further along the coast –
probably an unthinkable distance unless I was part of a
migrating tribe – I should eventually have found my way to
the great brochs of Ousedale and Dunbeath, and with no A9
to ease my journey!

So it would have been a lonely outpost, backing on to a
thickly forested hinterland with few neighbours, and
always under threat. Otherwise there would have been no
reason for these comfortable, well-off farmers and fishermen to build such strongholds. But at least there would
have been the sea, with its easy catch of seafood. Here I
have to stop myself, because while I look out from my own
'broch' with nothing but delight at the water below me, my
BC neighbours across the Dornoch Firth would surely have
eyed their pleasant seascape more cautiously. At the very
first sight of a not necessarily friendly vessel, they would
have hurried their cattle and all the community inside
those unscalable walls, and would have barred that heavy
wooden door. Much too early, of course, for the great, high
dragon prows of the Viking ships, but no doubt in 800 or
600 or 100 BC (or whenever the experts decide) there would
have been suspicious characters of some other kind.

A mile down the road from the Carn Liath Broch rises
the imposing, elegant structure, somewhat in the style of a
French château, of Dunrobin Castle. But what I see, as
distinct from what I am looking at, is not that vast, white,
turreted country seat, but walls that are dyed deep red –
red with the blood of the dispossessed, those sad victims of
the Clearances. For this is where it all started – eagerly
taken in hand, I admit with guilt and grief, by two
Englishmen, very much on the make and busying themselves with the lucrative task of substituting sheep for
men. Here was the beginning of that long tale of
disinheritance and expulsion and famine and pestilence and
death. And perhaps it is some small consolation to know
that it is another Englishman, John Prebble, who in his
book *The Highland Clearances* has told the story with a

burning clarity and compassion. Not that any book can make a restitution for what was done by the people of a particular countryside against their own people. This, to me, is the nub of the affair. In England, at that time, there was equal cruelty and exploitation, though different in kind. The English poor were necessary to industry and were therefore retained, to spend their lives in the coalmines or the 'dark Satanic mills'. Becoming so useful, they had the advantage, if it can be called that, of not being driven out. The peculiar dreadfulness of the Clearances lies precisely in the fact that the poor were no longer needed, even though they had lived for generations in the Highlands. So they had to go.

And go they did, transported in leaking vessels to America, often drowning as the worn-out ships foundered in mid-Atlantic. But while I see the white walls of Dunrobin as bright red, I realize that, for these later generations, they are the colour they appear to be. Just as today we cannot blame the youth of modern Germany for the sins of their Nazi grandparents, so we cannot blame today's Scottish landowners for what their forefathers did in the Clearances. Though it has to be said, also, that in the history of every family and nation, there is always an inescapable sharing, whether with pride or guilt, in what to us may be the past but which still reaches out to touch those who are living now.

This acceptance of being bound up with the past is very real to me, though not in this place and not for myself. I look back to another people who also were dispossessed, but with the certainty of death, rather than its likelihood, already implicit in their dispossession. The extinguishing of European Jewry arose out of acts undertaken for totally different reasons and with totally different aims from those which took place during the Clearances. Yet, in a queer way, there is a certain similarity in what happened, since both the Jewish and the Highland people were driven out of their own long-established homes by their own long-established neighbours, than which there is no greater or more final desolation. Here, as they both discovered, we have no abiding place. In the Clearances, those who died did so in their fired cabins, or beneath an insufficiently sheltering whin-bush on a bitter shore, or in those leaky boats. In the Holocaust, they died in the concentration camps and gas chambers of modern Europe; also in leaky boats which had conveyed them to a homeland from which the British turned them away.

During my growing up, there were several way-marks that led me towards a long involvement in Jewish affairs, one of them being in Germany in 1934 when I had accidentally got mixed up with a Nazi demonstration in Trier, finding myself in the main square, jammed between thousands of uniformed youngsters. From down the street a band approached, its music beating into the pulse; there was rhythmic shouting and a hypnotic flicker of torches. The tableaux rolled slowly past, lorries decked with swastikas, each paying its own tribute to the Führer, each followed by platoons of precision marchers.

And then it came: the roar from all those eager throats, the exultant *Heil Hitler!*, the click of heels, arms shooting stiffly skyward, the discharge of power. Again and again it resounded, the released creation greeting its saviour, plighting its troth with darkness. As the first dreadful cry burst from them, and the arms whipped into a slanting forest, I took a long, deep breath, staring fixedly at the shoulders of the young man in front of me, and slid my hands stubbornly into my mackintosh pockets. The glory and the triumph washed through these initiates, compelling, explosive, urgent. It caught their whole world together and made of them one dedicated offering. As for me, I stood there, obstinate as usual, my hands remaining pressed down, rammed hard into my pockets, clenched fiercely and in disgust as the hunger swept about me.

I think that were I asked to pick out one single moment in my life to which I can look back with relief and thankfulness, with a sense that, somehow, I had managed to preserve a necessary immunity, it would be that moment in Trier. There I instinctively made a rejection which – at that time in 1934 – I could not logically have justified, but none the less a repudiation which, had I not made it, would have pursued me ever afterwards with inexpiable guilt.

Later, I lay and shivered on my hotel bed, as the flares raced in reflected patterns across the ceiling and the shouting grew violent and uncurbed. As the night wore on, I could hear the stumbling of drunken feet below my window, the unsteady yelling of a liberated mob, the brief spurts of wild excitement rising and falling, now near, now far, as men ran through the streets as if searching. But, in search of what? At that time, I had no idea. It was not until 1936, when Victor Gollancz published his documentary *The Yellow Spot*, that I fully understood what was really happening in Nazi Germany. I knew then that, during the night of drunken rowdiness in Trier, as I lay wakeful and frightened, Jews would have been pulled out of their houses, perhaps just along the street, stripped of their belongings and, as in Gollancz's many accounts, left dead in a ditch or strung across a fence. Why is it that we do not hear the unspoken cry of terror? Why does our flesh remain a barrier against the endless screaming of another's mind? And, on that particular night in Trier, what in any case could I have done? There it is again. The same unanswerable question.

Now, as I stand upon the Dornoch shore, staring at that heavily burdened castle, I am seeing two tragedies: one, more than a century ago, which still haunts many a Highlander; the other, much nearer in time and haunting rather more people, including myself. The lesser tragedy of the Clearances, now over and done with, produced new generations building new lives in rather more responsive countries than their own. The greater dreadfulness of the

Holocaust, now over though by no means done with, has produced its own new homeland, though the Israel which partly arose out of the ashes of European Jewry can have, as yet, no certainty of ever becoming an abiding place.

12

Wolves and Horny Gollochs

A winter's day, a day when the sou'westerly that had blown around the house all night like a mighty sea is now sinking back exhausted, its last, slowly expiring breaths lashing the heavy Firth. Even at seven o'clock it is quite dark, giving one the impression that sunlight may never again touch this northern coast. In any case it will be two hours and six minutes before it is likely to do so, on this the darkest morning of the year.

The fire, banked down with peat for the night, has been awakened and is now in good heart, casting shadows and spurts of light around the Snug; glinting on the pictures; flickering over objects picked up from the shore, pebbles and odd-shaped bits of wood. It flows along the stretch of pale rush matting and over the spines of books. It catches a piece of black fossil fern, the fronds sharply delineated in the carbonized rock, a bit of earth's history that is 300 million years old. Some of the paintings are my own, inevitably of stones and stone circles, one of Edward caught as he stretched down his paw to take the long leap off the vegetable garden wall. The furniture is old, not valuable old but used old. The room is, I decide, sipping my first cup of tea and looking about me, warm and comfortable. What more could I wish for? Close to the fire are three armchairs, and I remember Thoreau's words: 'I had three chairs in my house; one for solitude, two for friendship, three for society.' This room had known all three, while the entire small house is filled with evidences of a rather earlier, indeed of a lifelong company of people.

Now it is nine o'clock, so I move to the window, hoping the sulky clouds will keep their distance so that I may watch that miraculous winter glimpse of the sun coming up behind the Moray hills. You wait endlessly, it seems, because of being afraid of missing it, while the scarlet clouds slowly fade to purple, then grey, till a paleness spreads across the orange-streaked horizon, paler and paler as the colour is washed away. And then it comes. Not as a rim of solid gold but, in that first magical moment, as a spark of fire, a sudden flash of brilliance. You see this only if the horizon is clear, and that is not so frequent. But when it happens, the result is breath-taking, like a great celestial torch switched on and off, following which the curve of the sun itself begins slowly to grow behind the hills. A good beginning to the day.

There's another good beginning when I enter the book-room at the front of the house and look out of the window. In front of me, about a hundred yards away and sitting quietly upon the winter-sown wheat, I see nine Whooper swans, resting after their long journey south. They will have come down from their breeding-grounds in Finland or Iceland, perhaps even from Russia or northern Asia. They come and go oblivious of frontiers and they carry no passports. Even though I stand inside the room, partly screened by the curtains, they have noticed me, thin necks straightening at once in a signal of alarm. But it seems they cannot be bothered to move; the faint shadow that attracted their attention appears now to have gone away. The necks come down again, reassured, and without moving their heavy white bodies they go on cropping young shoots and other delicacies such as, here and there, an unlucky worm.

Within a few minutes I hear a creaking of wings and five more swans come in from the north. They are, as so often after take-off from somewhere near at hand, still flying low, perhaps only twenty feet from the ground, but they

have no intention of landing again and take no notice of
their brothers and sisters on this tempting field. Very soon
they begin to rise, thrusting upward with outstretched
necks and slow beat of great wings, and becoming, in a
sudden gleam of sunlight, five shining patches of snow
sailing against the sky. They disappear in a haphazard
straggle towards their usual wintering along the Cromarty
Firth. Minutes later, when I return to the window, the field
is empty and the nine resting swans have moved on to join
them.

This is clearly a day for outdoors. So I ignore the
washing, the vacuum cleaner and the dirty, storm-
smeared windows, sticky with sand and salt. But I cannot
ignore Halley, now highly suspicious, knowing at once that
she is not included on this expedition. I explain matters as
persuasively as I can, but she flounces through the cat-flap
and away to kill something – anything – just to show me
where I get off. No doubt I shall return to a row of little
corpses, laid neatly at the back door, with a complacent cat
watching from beneath a bush and extracting the maximum
satisfaction from my distress.

Setting off for the shore, I first make a morning recce on
the edge of the cliff. There I find that the sea is lumbering
around, heavy and dark grey, with top breakers rolling in
white foam far out across the Firth, and long rollers
building up against the rocks. There are, however, shafts
of that earlier sun, and a strong wind seems to be attending
to some obstructive clouds. I watch the shore and am
rewarded. Undoubtedly shearwaters! Several of them,
swift and dark, doing their own thing of expertly shearing
the incoming breakers. The sea heaves itself up; the wave
curls over; a gleam of sun catches the smooth inner curve,
rich green as the crest begins to topple. But the shearwaters
are ready, banking in rapid flight and literally scooping
along inside the tunnel of water moments before it
collapses, when they shoot upwards to the sky a split
second before the frothy mountain crashes on to the rocks.

I cannot be certain, as they stiffly wheel and flash, whether they are great or Cory's shearwaters, but possibly the former: a pelagic bird belonging with the fulmars to the same order as the petrels, but, unlike fulmars, not often seen close to land. They breed in the Tristan da Cunha Islands and range over immense distances from the South Atlantic as far as Iceland and Greenland. This is the only time I have seen them, and again it is the story of sighting a distress flare: either you happen to be in the right place at the right time, or you don't. I watch them until they skim rapidly away, rather ordinary brownish birds but bringing with them the lure of vast oceans.

Another bird appears this morning before I leave the cliff. Far out to sea I glimpse something sharply white among the blown crests of waves: a large bird with black-tipped wings. It is too distant and flying too low for me to be sure of it at first, even with binoculars, but then I realize it is a gannet. Its size and shape settle the matter, since gannets are about a yard long with a narrow head which slopes without forehead into a stout, pointed beak. In flight, the front of the bird almost seems to match the back, giving the body that cigar shape which distinguishes it from any other sea-bird. It is the most spectacular diver when fishing, comes to the land only to breed, and, though sometimes seen with others of its kind, it will more usually be solitary or be found in twos. I watched it eagerly as it grew smaller and smaller, its brilliant whiteness eventually smudged against the flurry of white waves. Then it was gone, and I turned to the cliff path.

I had a particular reason, that morning, for seeking the shore. A long way off, in one of the stubble fields bordering the cliff towards the lighthouse, I had noticed a large gathering of dark, heavy bodies: greylag geese flighting in to this part of Scotland as winter visitors. Like the swans, they would probably have come from Iceland, or it may have been from either Scandinavia or Macedonia. Greylags are the largest of the 'grey geese', not perhaps so dramatic as some, but softly greyish brown and wonderfully striped by reason of the white frilly edges to their wing and body feathers. Their legs are pinkish. Their bills are bright orange. Nowadays they are fairly well known through the studies of Konrad Lorenz, and quite often large flocks can easily be seen as they graze in open country. The difficulty about watching them at close quarters is that, having no cover from their feeding-grounds, they are easily intimidated, while the sentries posted on the fringes of the flock are experts at their job.

So I planned a detour, hoping to arrive back on the cliff-top at the place where I could lie hidden by bushes of whin, nicely serving as a hide. The geese were not likely to stay long, this being only a feeding patch, so I hurried along the shore, resisting the temptation to linger, and eventually went up a narrow cart-track, long since disused, which brought me to within a few yards of my quarry. Nearing the crest of the cliff, I lay down flat on my stomach, inching my way up the last few yards, well hidden behind the whin. Since whin is evergreen and always impenetrable, this meant that I could see nothing at all, so I had cautiously to raise my head and reveal myself.

There must have been two or three hundred of them, all voraciously feeding on grasses and the remains of the barley harvest. The flock itself took no notice of me, but at once certain long necks reared high as the sentries swung round to carry out an inspection. I flattened myself, burrowing into the mud and litter of the cliff-top so that they could not see my face. After a while I looked again, covering my skin with gloved hands and peering through the fingers. But the sentries were not to be deceived. Now fully alerted and facing me squarely, their alarm communicated itself to the whole beautiful, peaceful flock. A restlessness swept over them as if they shared a common mind and had been told simultaneously that it was time to move on. So they moved, fast. There was a moment of confusion, a blur of grey and white and pink and orange, the quick stretching of a multitude of necks and wings, the creaking whir of bodies as they rose swiftly and easily as puffs of grey smoke, darkening the sky for an instant as if whipping open a large umbrella. Then, with long necks thrusting forward, they swept away to a more propitious feeding-ground. I jumped to my feet as they left, watching as they mounted the air currents, not in their migrating V formation but separated into irregular groups and heading, I thought, towards a large sheet of inland water, a bird sanctuary called Loch Eye, which no doubt they had made their temporary headquarters. Would they stay over, or would they push further south towards African wintering grounds? I had no idea. I should never know anything about their lives, except to rejoice that they were utterly free. I hoped they would escape being shot.

Down on the shore the morning was yet young, and I sat on a rock eating a Mars bar. The small pools, ever refreshed by the incoming tide, were crystal clear, with a sediment of ground-up shells at the bottom. Racing clouds and patches of blue sky were reflected in the rock shadows, and I remembered with some amusement that it was not the bright pools such as now lay at my feet but drains and dirty gutters which first taught me what natural beauty was all about. I must have been thirteen at the time, and busy devouring Ruskin with passionate devotion. I had come, incredulous, to the passage in *Modern Painters* where the master declaims that 'there is hardly a road-side pond or pool which has not as much landscape *in* it as above it. It is not the brown, muddy, dull thing we suppose it to be . . . nay, the ugly gutter, that stagnates over the drain bars . . . is not altogether base. If you will look deep enough, you may see the dark, serious blue of far-off sky, and the passing of pure clouds. It is at your own will that you see in that despised stream either the refuse of the street, or the image of the sky'.

So I had hastened out, for gutters are much the same everywhere. I remember squatting down on the pavement,

rather as I used to search for my stones, peering at a sheet
of dirty water where dead leaves and fragmented bits of
paper clogged a drain. You could distinguish the iron bars
upon, so to speak, the sea-bed. In fact it was a slimy,
unsightly place. And yet, if you refocused your eyes, you
saw at once that everything could have quite a different
appearance. There, indeed, moved the fleecy clouds; there,
the deep blue of furthest sky; there, the dark lacework of
trees: all mirrored in that brown, stagnating puddle. It was a
revelation which never left me, which sent me scurrying
home to pursue Ruskin, purple passages and all, with total
dedication. Later I recognized the danger of that luxuriant
prose and struggled to resist it, well knowing that I might
too easily be carried away. But the knowledge that it was
with my own will that I must look around me, must
distinguish, must actually *see* what I was seeing, has
remained with me, ineradicably.

So now I enjoyed the rock pools, clambering over the
sandstone reefs, scrabbling in the water for pebbles to take
home. The entire Tarbat Ness shoreline offers the most
extraordinary small stones; ridged, no doubt volcanically,
into curious designs and marked with precise bands of
contrasting colour, so that I could conclude no walk without
collecting an increasingly weighty load to add to the
already overcrowded window-sills. I also sorted through
the piles of broken fish-boxes and bits of rough wood
scattered along the shore during the storm, pouncing on
suitable lengths to make into picture frames. The shore
always has an endless supply of useful treasures. Moreover,
if you sit quietly for a long time – not exactly congenial in
winter but there are always sheltering rocks – you can
observe a variety of bird life apart from the gulls and
fulmars. Cormorants and the small shags abound along the
coast, both so heraldic, looking like left-overs from
prehistoric times, particularly when they stand bolt upright
on a rock with their angular wings spread wide to dry in the
wind. A necessary exercise, since they do not secrete the oil

that enables the feathers of other birds to resist saturation by sea-water. They skim closely over the waves, and, after diving, all that can be seen is a thin black little neck and head travelling along the surface, looking like the periscope of a miniature submarine. Once, with a friend, I found a dead shag wedged into the cleft of a rock. We had been attracted to it by its mate which was perched disconsolately beside it, refusing to stir until we were just inches away and then retiring only a short distance. It showed no fear of us, just a huddled indifference, eyeing us with that remote, blank coldness common to all birds, yet contriving, with its ruffled feathers, to look inexpressibly deprived. We beat a hasty retreat, overcome by our obvious intrusion into grief, leaving the mourning shag in quiet possession of its dead.

Among the assorted bird-life of the cliff and shore are several birds of prey: kestrels, hovering for minutes at a time in one exact spot whatever wind is blowing, and then dropping like a stone on to some unwary small creature; also hen-harriers and sometimes, if you are fortunate enough to see it, that rare winter visitor, the rough-legged buzzard. Usually it will be perched on a fence-post, grey and tall, its feathery legs looking like a cowboy's chaps. Rather understandably, it never lets you get near, but as it soars into the sky you have that wonderful sight of its great spread wings, the tips separated like an eagle's into long, dark, curving fingers. Best of all, so far as I am concerned, is the lapwing, that crazy acrobat of birds, black and white and metal green, wobbly in flight and given to falling out of the sky, plunging and twisting, wings flapping as if out of control, turning somersaults and seeming, to your alarm, about to hit the earth before it swoops up again in a hairbreadth escape. A display flight which must surely captivate its watching mate!

Birds and beasts! The sea, the shore, the cliff are crowded with them, and it is easy to overlook the legions of smaller creatures living out their more hidden lives within or underneath the tangled vegetation of raised beach and cliff-top: a whole world of energetic and scarcely recognized inhabitants to which we are totally unable to relate. They are aware of us only as interferers from whom, if touched, they flinch, each in its own appropriate fashion. But they are very much there. If I walk across the garden at dusk on a soft, warm, damp summer evening when the turf is moist and spongy, it is difficult to know where to put my feet, as I try to avoid treading on that most sizeable monster of the slug family, the large black. Dozens of them will be prowling among the grasses, feeding on anything they can find, preferably rotting leaves. On these occasions, I tell myself smugly, it is just as well the garden is a wild place, since a tidy garden, devoid of decaying plants and fungi, will drive the slug population to raid the lettuces instead. The large black does little damage in any case, but if picked up is better handled with a rag or piece of soft paper, since the sticky mucus it secretes is astonishingly adhesive and can be scrubbed off the fingers only with great difficulty and after many painful scourings. They tend, at a human touch, to contract into a small black blob, looking, as Michael Chinery somewhat disquietingly expresses it, 'like an animated prune'.* They take over the garden at night, but, like the *Sithe* who vanish at dawn into the hollow hills, withdraw silently below the earth as the sun rises, or curl up in certain rocky fastnesses, so that early walks across the dewy grass will reveal only one or two stragglers, carelessly lagging behind.

Insects, too, are well established here. There are the ladybirds, to be discovered in dense, huddled clumps of several hundred, packed tightly together in well-chosen corners of shed or garden fence as they begin their autumn hibernation. Even more familiar is the company of a myriad horny gollochs, better known down south

---

* *The Natural History of the Garden* (Collins, 1977).

as earwigs. These I have enjoyed since childhood, when they lived in a creeper beside the bedroom window. Having a strange passion for anything white (strange because it affords no camouflage) they regularly explored the crevices of white sheets and pillow-cases and, since they never actually seemed interested in my ears, I would drift off to sleep while watching as they scaled the bedclothes' humps or dropped into their hollows. Up here and dignified as horny gollochs, they seem particularly fascinated by the whiteness of the freezer, queuing patiently along the top edge in hopes, presumably, of getting inside. But when the moment comes and the door is opened, they lose their footing and plunge headlong down the sheer, shining cliff.

Most intriguing of all these small local residents are those magical hunters, the wolf spiders. I remember looking out of the window one summer evening, puzzled by what I saw as the sun slanted across some rough mounds of ancient field dung and nettles. For, draped over the taller weeds, stretched in cloudy canopies along the tops of single grasses, and secured by thin silken ropes, there had appeared a tented encampment, delicately miniature, pale and insubstantial, and looking like enchanted pavilions conjured by the *Sithe* to house their evening revels. In actual fact, as I had discovered when I went out to investigate, they were the nurseries of the *Pisaura mirabilis*, one of the more exotic branches of the wolf spider family, a name truly meriting its translation of wonderful, extraordinary, marvellous. The mother *mirabilis*, having laboriously dragged her egg cocoon around until it is about to hatch, will fasten it carefully to a leaf and spin a roomy tent around it. Within the enveloping safety of this gauze-like structure a teeming multitude of pin-head young will emerge, and there they will spend their first few days while the mother sits on guard outside. Later the new generation will set up house not in silken tents but in silken caves sited beneath stones or logs – another echo of the hollow hills.

On this particular evening I had remained watching for

nearly an hour as the sun went down and the soft white
veils blew gently to and fro, yet never tearing, while inside,
perfectly secure within what appeared to be such a fragile
home, tiny brown specks detached themselves from the
edges of the compact central mass and busily scampered
up and down the transparent walls of their nursery.
Mirabilis indeed!

13

The Mincing Machine

At home there were no little corpses to trip over, though Halley was still pointedly absent. So, on the principle of its being as well to be hanged for a sheep as a lamb, I take a quick snack and go off to disentangle my moped from the shed at the bottom of the track. Thence to the lighthouse, beyond which I walk along a heathery path for a few hundred yards and come at last to Tarbat's 'nose'. Here is the actual point, the sloping fringe of rocks beyond which there is not much to stop me reaching the North Pole, given perhaps a polar bear or two, as well as a few icebergs. Against this flat reef the North Sea beats relentlessly, dividing itself to thrust left and right into the Dornoch and Moray Firths. It is always blowy on the Ness, a boisterous argument between wind and water, punctuated by the kittiwakes' constant refrain and the wilder screams of sea-gulls. I am almost surrounded by water, the land now left behind and only the shelving sandstone rocks beneath my feet. It is the end of the world. The end of my world. Beyond is only a vast open waste of sea, with, to the west, a long, pale receding coastline backed by disappearing mountains.

Many strange things have happened around Tarbat's nose. In May 1809 the sailing-packet from Burghead, bearing those two English adventurers to their work of destruction in the Clearances, would have passed by on its way to Sutherland and Dunrobin Castle. Later, anyone standing here could have watched a monument being

erected to the Duke of Sutherland on a hill above
Dunrobin, said to be a tribute to his having shot his seven
hundredth stag. Unfortunately the pillar is clearly visible
from my front windows. Further back, in the eleventh
century, there would have been that battle on Tarbat Ness
between one part of Earl Thorfinn's competent army and
the rather less effective invading force of the King of Alba.
Thorfinn's ultimate victory, achieved over a wide front
which extended as far as Dingwall, is thought to have been
greatly assisted by St Duthac, the local saint, both by his
holy admonitions and by his excellent swordsmanship.

Still further back, perhaps between AD 400 and 900, the
whole north-east of Scotland, including Tarbat Ness,
would have known the Picts, that mysterious people
probably descended from Iron Age or even from Bronze or
Stone Age tribes. They left no translatable written records
but dotted the landscape with magnificent monoliths
bearing incised or carved symbols whose meaning is still
only to be guessed at. The earliest stones, known as Class I
and erected before the Picts were Christianized, are
roughly hewn but with the Pictish symbols precisely and
elegantly engraved. A later grouping, Class II, is composed
of tall, thin, rectangular slabs carrying both the ancient
symbols and the Christian cross; while in Class III only the
cross remains and the early symbols have, alas, been
forgotten – or forbidden.

More than two hundred of these Pictish stones have
been discovered, some still standing in their original place,
others now to be found in Scottish museums. They are
unique to Scotland, the artistic treasure of a people whose
language is lost. And it is not the later cross-slabs,
beautifully carved as they are, which so provoke our
interest, but those unshaped earlier stones, sharing between
them a total of about twenty designs, each stone bearing
perhaps two or four of the symbols. We are forced to guess
at their meaning, and the guesses have ranged from
suggestions that the monoliths, mostly standing solitary in

a grazing field or surrounded by ploughed land, were erected as boundary or battlefield markers, or that they were gravestones, or even that they united the symbols of certain families as marriage stones. It seems that the problem is still open for solution. Therefore, in presenting my own theory, I can feel free to speculate, also to reject previous suggestions. I believe the Picts had not simply evolved a set of family symbols appropriate to the particular age they were living in. I think they were looking back, far back into their past, and that, while the designs were in use from about AD 500 until they were displaced by the cross, their meaning was rooted in the distant beginnings of Pictish history. There are two kinds of symbols: one of birds and beasts; the other of more abstract designs such as rods and zigzags, circles and crescents, circular dishes with handles, mirrors and combs. All these point back to certain objects considered by neolithic and later peoples as vitally important or magic or holy. It is significant that almost every design has its counterpart in the literature of myth and fairy or folk-tale. The animals and birds depicted are serpent, fish, goose, eagle, wolf, bull, horse, stag, cow and boar, well-known enchanted beasts appearing again and again in early folk-tales. The magic cauldron of the Celts, the sorcerer's rod, the divine sun and moon, and indeed the comb and mirror (so often thrown behind an escaping hero and heroine, to become dense forest and hindering lake to bar the giant's pursuit), all these are powerful magic objects known to every reader of fairy-tales. Others are not so easy to identify, and maybe by AD 500 the Picts had developed some new magic.

It is not necessarily the modern scientific investigator who comes up with a clue to the truth. The symbols have led to much argument, mirror and comb being considered by some as perhaps signifying a woman of importance in a tribe. But this is doubtful. In the mid-nineteenth century that great gatherer of Scottish 'popular tales', Campbell of Islay, noted and discussed the high incidence of magic

combs and mirrors, and indeed of every shining metal
object, in the ancient stories he uncovered and collected.
He considered this to be the result of neolithic man's
amazement at the sophisticated domestic and battle equipment brought for trading by the discoverers of bronze, so
that, for a simpler people, such eventually ordinary artefacts
were immediately endowed with magic power and mystery,
valued as being in themselves objects of veneration.
Campbell saw the comb as having been in prehistoric times
'always a coveted object worth great exertions, and often
magical'. He also studied the Pictish stone now in the
museum of Dunrobin Castle, 'on which a comb is carved
with other curious devices which have never been ex-
plained'. He did not, it seems, make the connection that the
Dunrobin comb, as all the Pictish combs, together with the
magical beasts and those other 'curious devices' were allied
to the 'coveted objects' of his folk-tales, being, as it were,
the outward and visible signs of the ancient tales handed
down from generation to generation and having their
roots in a neolithic culture.

I have learnt much from Campbell's insight and careful
scholarliness, and it seems clear to me that these mysterious
and exquisitely incised monoliths must have served as
spell-stones. Each would probably have been erected in the
midst of a small community, much as a market cross used
to be the centre of a medieval village. They would have
been both magical and holy, and I would suggest that their
function was to provide a strong protective force for the
well-being of a family or tribe. The Picts would have been
expressing, in their own uncertain world, the remembered
cravings of their ancestors for things which were 'out of
this world', things that could subjugate others by the force
of their enchantment and, therefore, things of power.
Today, in words rather than in artefacts, all these potent
symbols still litter the pages of every book of folk-tales.

Later the Christian cross was to be accepted as also a
magic protection. It too would take its place (carved then

rather than incised) upon carefully shaped stones. Soon it would begin to be given precedence, placed boldly on the face of the stone, while the older symbols were crowded on to the back. Eventually only the cross would survive.

But the comb and the mirror, the talking birds and beasts, the magician's wand, the enchanted cauldron, these also proclaim the universal need for magical protection, arising, for the early Picts, out of ancient superstition and satisfied by the creation of venerated objects. The thing done (that is, the idea translated into tactile, visible stone) brings about the thing desired. When I walk in the field at Edderton, some miles from where I live, and look across to the great pointed stone bearing its fish symbol and several other 'curious devices' as it stands solitary in the dusk, I am aware that it is more than just a boundary marker or the witness to a marriage contract, or the site of a battle. It has to be the protecting genius of the place, armed with enchantment to keep at bay the powers of darkness.

The Picts, like those earlier builders of Carn Liath across the Dornoch Firth and like the even earlier neolithic people who, with Corrimony and other cairns, put up some of the earliest stone structures in Britain, would have had a hard time of it in a far from friendly climate. Even as late as the eighteenth century both Sutherland and the Ness on which I was now standing were part of a wilderness described by John Prebble as being 'a wasteheap of the glacial age'. And it is to that last Ice Age that the Ness inevitably draws us, for the very rocks of that shelving point would have seen the light only after the great weight of the ice-sheets had melted away. There they now lie, ground down and fissured by ice and wind and water. There were mammals living here between the later Ice Ages, reindeer and elk, woolly rhinoceros and mammoth. And it was well before the close of the last Ice Age, without their even waiting for it to end, that living creatures moved in and took over, as so vividly outlined by Dr W. H. Murray: 'Nothing in the Highland story is more astonishing than the speed with which wildlife moved into the emptied land at least 4000 years before the close of the Ice Age, and, despite the withering cold of winters longer than now, held its ground.'*

It became a land with a plant cover of heath and birch copses, and by 12000 BC 'three brown butterflies had arrived'. After this there was no stopping the tide of animal life which joined their fragile forerunners: again the reindeer and great elk; even the aurochs, that fantastic wild ox standing over six feet high with a horn-span of about two yards. There were stoats (Ah, Edward, why did I lead you on?), hares, brown bears, lemmings and voles, followed by a whole host of otters, foxes, weasels, wild cats, badgers and hedgehogs, not to mention horses. The geese and swans I had watched that morning would, even then, have settled here after their flight from the Arctic, though they would not have journeyed further south.

After about 7000 BC, and during the next two thousand years of wet, warm weather, vast forests would have taken over the land. They survived. But the inter-glacial forests, which once had covered the North Sea basin, lay drowned beneath the rising ice-waters. It makes one bitterly sad to realize, on reading Murray's account, that with the coming of neolithic man, who killed off the northern lynx, we began our own long human history of wildlife decimation. One by one those earlier 'pilgrims', who had chosen to go 'always a little further', and who had indeed blazed the trail for mankind, have been extinguished.

So here I stand today, yet partly in those earlier times, taking great gulps of blustery air and wandering among the rocks. I think back to my arrival at this house on the cliff. Since then I have absorbed a lot of things, taking them into

---

* *Wildlife of Scotland*, ed. Fred Holliday (Macmillan, 1979).

me rather like an old-fashioned mincing machine with a handle at the side. I turn the little handle round and round, rapidly and enthusiastically mincing together everything as it comes flooding in, but then shaping it deliberately into something which makes an acceptable pattern. Life on a cliff-top is varied, the wildlife being far more numerous than the human beings who inhabit it, and, as we see, far longer established. Those animals and birds which appeared here long before we humans showed our faces, they were the first-comers. It is their place as much as, if not more than, it is ours. We naturally do not always agree with this. Perhaps it is because we are the late arrivals that we are so tenacious about our tenancy. For that is what it is: we are tenants, not owners. We own nothing. We come with empty hands and we go with empty hands.

Many years ago I 'owned' a very old cottage. That is, I held certain pieces of paper called 'deeds'. But, though I had paid out money in exchange for those pieces of paper, I could never believe with any confidence that the cottage was 'mine'. How could I, a transient human being, 'own' a building which had stood for so many centuries, saturated with so much history? How could I 'possess' a plot of earth, consider as belonging to me a portion of the planet, however small? Did I, then, own that chestnut tree? Or possess the honeysuckle? And what of the fox which used the garden as a short-cut home? At most I could call myself a kind of watch-dog, to make sure they got on all right. An American Indian wrote that 'if all the beasts were gone, man would die from great loneliness of spirit'. So it all goes much deeper than the desirability (for whom?) of conserving a particular dying species, or of preserving, at long last, the trees by whose breathing we ourselves are enabled to breathe, or even of the practical need to restore the earth-encircling atmosphere into which we are busy poking holes. It is an exploration of a more fundamental kind, leading to an acceptance of what our tenancy of this planet implies. Meanwhile, as pointers on the way, the lonely shag is seen to mourn for his dead mate. The dolphins plan the rescue of a human in distress. The seal regards you from his own world, reaching out, if you also make an overture, to touch your reality. The sea-gull, vicious and predatory, relates in long sweeps of companionable flight around your head.

I am back home again, and Halley has rapidly disposed of a placating bowl of fish. She does not hang on to her grievances. We begin to think about the evening's activities, one of us inclined to a good read, the other to the serious business of night hunting. I look at Halley. She is sitting on the floor, thoughtfully nibbling at her toes, always an important preparation. A proficient huntswoman never neglects the cleaning of her weapons. 'What do you think of it all?' I ask her, and she looks up instantly, squeezing her eyes together in what she knows to be a fetching little cat-smile, just in case I don't remember that there's still room for more fish. I ignore this. 'I mean Life, the Universe and Everything.' She yawns. I can see her attention is wandering, so I raise my voice a little. 'The Cosmos,' I tell her sternly. 'Have you considered the Cosmos?'

But no, she hasn't. Nor does she wish to. However, she is aware that I am on about something, so, following the age-old cat precept of 'when in doubt, wash', she licks an industrious paw and begins wiping behind her ears. Clearly there will be another storm tonight. I sigh. Edward, of course, knew about Life. And the Universe. And, indeed, about Everything.